VIHORROR!

Cocktales of Sex and Death

Will Viharo

Seattle, WA

VIHORROR! Cocktales of Sex and Death

Copyright 2020 Will Viharo

Any similarities between the characters of this book and any persons, alive or dead, may or may not be intentional.

Cover design by Dyer Wilk

Formatting by Rik – WildSeasFormatting.com

ISBN-13: 978-0-578-63799-0

First Printing
Printed in the United States of America
Published by Thrillville Press
www.thrillville.net

COCKTALE MENU

DISMEMBER ME   1
The half-naked woman was running from something she couldn't remember down a dark street in a place she didn't recognize.

THE LOST SOCK   11
Everything you do feels like an act of desperation. Even something as simple as doing your laundry.

NIGHTMARE CLOUD   27
Life for the lonely man had become like a dream when the dreamer realizes it's a dream, so nothing seemed to matter because none of it would last, because none of it was real.

DEAD NUDES   39
The stripper parked directly in front of the club where she danced. If Luck was a lady, then she was wet and ready for entry. But Luck was taking the night off.

MOOD MASSACRE   50
"Fuck you and the whore you rode in on," she told him just before she shot his dick off. It was already a hell of a honeymoon.

SLAUGHTER OF THE SENSES   63
The naked bodies of her dead lovers were buried in the basement of her callous conscience. But so what? They didn't deserve her anyway, much less their own lives.

HUNT, KILL, FEED, FUCK. REPEAT.   142

The creatures followed only their primal instincts in pursuit of their own short term survival, fornicating without propagation, existing without living, oblivious to the raging nightmares inevitably replacing their complacent little dreams.

For All the Anonymous People
And the Animals

"I don't know why people expect art to make sense.
They accept the fact that life doesn't make sense."
— *David Lynch*

.

DISMEMBER ME

The half-naked woman was running from something she couldn't remember down a dark street in a place she didn't recognize.

She ran into a movie theater called the Paramount with a neon-lit marquee that read *Kiss Me Deadly*. Without even stopping to buy a ticket, she walked briskly past the box office kiosk and into the vast chamber where black and white images from long ago flickered in the dark like a drunken flashback.

On the screen, a woman wearing only an overcoat was running down the middle of a highway, in the middle of the night. A sharp-dressed detective in a sports car caught up with her. She was escaping from a local asylum. "Remember me," she said to him.

That's when the woman clutched her own overcoat and realized she too was nude beneath the loose-fitting garment. Her feet were bare and dirty. Her throat ached and she felt wan and weak.

The theater was nearly empty so hardly anyone noticed her. A flashlight illuminated the presence of an usher, who requested to see the woman's ticket. Since she had none to produce, she fled past him and back out into the nocturnal vortex.

A beat-up 1950s-era cab that looked like an automotive zombie with shark fins screeched to a halt and instinctively she climbed into the back. The style of the vehicle differed from all others parked on the street. It was like something out of the movie.

"Where to?" the cabbie asked.

"I don't know," she said. "Anywhere."

"Well, I gotta check back into the station, so just come with me and we'll figure it out, all right?"

"Okay." She had no choice but to trust in this stranger, whom she could hear but not fully see. Only the back of his bulky head was visible in the blackness. At least he provided transportation and sanctuary.

During the drive the cabbie took a call from his scratchy dispatch radio, which sounded like it was transmitting messages from another era. He just listened to the mysterious voice on the other end and then said "okay" before hanging up. Then he turned on the radio. "Love You So" by Ron Holden was playing, obviously on AM, sounding scratchy and remote, as if beamed from another time and place, beyond or behind them.

Finally he pulled up at the Tacoma Yellow Cab Company. The sign was part of a large, cartoonish replica of an old school cabbie head on top of the roof. It reminded her of the Bob's Big Boy statue or the floats at the Macy's Thanksgiving Parade, she realized, even though at the moment she didn't know the meaning of any of those words and so didn't get her own mental references. In any case, it gave her the creeps. She noticed the door number and street sign designating the location as 3101 S. 36th Street. That didn't solve any mysteries or answer any questions about her own identity. No miracle on this street.

The cabbie got out and looked inside the back-seat window. He was still just a misshapen silhouette in the moonlight. "I'm going to go grab my lunch, then I'll take you where you need to go."

"But I don't know where I need to go."

"You don't need to know, because I do. Be right

back."

The cabbie went inside the building beneath the giant, grotesque head wearing a cabbie hat. It seemed to be watching her. Suddenly she realized how cold she was in the crisp evening air. She pulled the overcoat tighter around her body, which was shapely and shivering.

A few moments later the cabbie returned with a steel lunchbox that appeared to be dripping a strange, red substance. It made her hungry and thirsty at once. He returned to the driver's seat, popped open the pail, opened a thermos, and offered her a sip. She accepted. The liquid was thick and salty and very satisfying. It dripped down her chin and beneath her coat. She wiped it from her cleavage and licked her fingers as the cabbie watched her in the rear-view mirror, fondling himself out of view. The lunchbox was apparently empty except for the thermos.

"Go ahead," he said. "Finish it. You need it more than I do."

She did. He started the cab and drove off as she guzzled the crimson beverage, which rejuvenated her energy and clarified her thoughts.

He dropped her off at a bar/restaurant called the Zodiac Supper Club. The address was 1116 Martin Luther King Jr. Way. That still didn't ring any mental bells. She never heard of this Martin fellow.

She went inside and sat at the bar, which ensconced in gothic, occult pop cultural artifacts that meant nothing to her. But her sartorial state attracted the wrong kind of attention. Esquivel was playing on the sound system. She didn't recognize the Space Age lounge music, but she found it spiritually soothing, especially given her predicament.

A handsome man in a sharp suit who oddly resembled the vintage screen detective she'd just seen sat next to her, his face a blur like a newspaper in a dream. "You're hot, and you're attracting my heat-seeking missile. What do you think of that?"

"If I say, 'You don't want to know,' I think that tells you all you need to know."

"You're not friendly. That's okay. Neither am I. I tend to only like people that don't like people, too."

"I don't like anybody, including you." If she knew anything, she knew that.

She looked at his throat. She could smell the masculine flesh, the strong cologne on the surface as well as the blood pulsing beneath.

"Let's go out back," she said with strangely calm confidence, taking his hand, emboldened by the suddenly realized power of her own seductive skills.

He nodded and followed her without question, as if it were all preordained. Once back there, out of sight, she opened her coat and let him in. He groped and kissed her breasts and reached down and felt her warm, wet vagina. She unzipped his pants and took his large member into her mouth and guzzled its gooey emissions which exploded all over her face and body. She wiped and lapped up the excess but it wasn't enough. She needed more.

With a sudden burst of strength she threw him again the alley wall and savagely bit into his jugular vein. The geyser of blood shot out and spewed over them both, but she was able to consume enough to further embolden and enrich her. Between the two bodily fluids she now felt almost completely restored.

Except for her memory. All she knew was that despite the nourishment, she only wanted to die.

Her volunteer victim slumped to the ground, fully drained and apparently dead. She fled, filled with his life essence and her own envy of his violent demise at her merciless hands.

Once again she found herself wandering down the dark streets of a town called Tacoma, a place she had never been or heard of, as far as she knew. But when she thought about it, she couldn't identify any particular place. She possessed no cognizant context for the world around her. It was as if she had just been born.

The overcoat was now sticky and stained with the stranger's bodily substances. The scent of both combined was intoxicating. She wanted more. Needed more.

The fat, faceless cabbie pulled up and picked her up again. "Love You So" was still playing on the radio, apparently in a loop. She noticed, but barely, distracted by her own urgent, increasingly cryptic dilemma.

"Where to now?" she asked.

"Does it matter?"

"No. Just feed me. Please."

"Coming right up."

The cabbie took her to a bus stop where a pretty young girl with long black hair and ivory skin was waiting for a ride home from work. Instead the woman motioned her into the backseat with her.

"Can we share the fare?" the young girl asked. "I'm pretty broke. I just have this bus pass. I'm a waitress. In fact, I think I saw you where I work earlier tonight, with that man. But then you both disappeared. How funny is fate?"

The woman didn't know what any of that meant, but the cabbie answered for her. "Hop in, honey, it's on us," he said. "Consider it a tip for the service you never had a chance to give. Till now."

Twenty minutes later the girl's nude, lifeless, drained body was casually dumped into Puget Sound. The cabbie had violated her corpse once the woman had finished feeding.

"I want to die," the woman said. "And yet I'm so hungry for what gives me life."

"Survival instinct," the cabbie said with a shrug.

"But why? What's the point? Living to take innocent life? This must be a nightmare. If only I could just wake up..."

"That's how it works, sweetie. The world, that is. I didn't make the rules and neither did you, so lighten up. At least you're on top of the food chain now. And you're a sexy woman. In any version of this thing called life, people that look like you always get to skip to the start of the line. Me, I've always been a loser. Until that one night I picked up this prissy fancy-pants European prick from SeaTac and everything changed. Don't get me wrong, I'm not complaining. I'm grateful. This snooty fairy not only gave me this gift, but he took me around a bit and taught me how to take advantage of it. He made me more, how should I say...sophisticated. I actually began reading books instead of just watching porn with my cat, who is now dead, my first meal, in fact. I still have that same basic lifestyle, only I work graveyard shifts now. Ultimately, no matter what happens to us, in the end we are who we are, am I right? Except now I'm who I was before plus way more, forever. Even though I'm still a disgusting piece of shit, I get pretty much whatever I want and need. Because I just take it. Before this one fateful fare, I was just some schlub rubbing one off in the coffee shop bathroom in between passengers, perpetually horny and lonely. I resorted to hookers but even they were disgusted by me. They had grown weary of my little old head burrowing into their beavers, wheezing and snorting, then rutting with unrestrained flatulence. Now none of it matters. See what I'm sayin'? No matter how bad it was before, it will all be better now."

The woman felt an internal vacuum where her soul should've been. Despite her ravenous appetite and voracious feasting she still felt discontent. Not just physically, but spiritually, where it hurt most.

But that was the problem, she suddenly realized. There was no nurturing the aching, gnawing pain, no matter how many she killed and consumed.

"I can't die, can I?" she asked the cabbie.

He shrugged. "I'm not your shrink. You killed him, actually. Just like the guy back at the Zodiac Club, who was one of ours, by the way. He was sent there to help."

"One of our what?"

"Union. Network. Tribe. Team. Club. Whatever."

"He sacrificed himself?"

The cabbie laughed. "I don't think that's what he'd call it. You're a good lookin' dame. He'd have nailed you without anyone asking. He did make a blood donation. But that's okay. He immediately replenished."

"You mean…he's not dead?"

"Not in the way you're wishing, no. You want me

to show you?"

"Yes."

"Okay."

The cabbie drove back to the Zodiac. Down the block they both saw her recent victim stumbling along. They stopped next to him. His face was ghastly, his pupils milky white, his flesh ashen. He drooled and lunged at the cab, but couldn't get in. Then the woman noticed another waitress from the Zodiac was lying on the sidewalk, motionless and disheveled. The man stopped clawing at the cab window and returned to his meal while it was still fresh.

"Horrible," she whispered.

"Don't be a hypocrite," the cabbie said as he continued driving. "You just did the same thing to him. The difference is, he was already one of us."

"I don't understand."

"You will."

"Why can't I remember? Why?"

"Because you blacked out after I attacked you," the cabbie said. "I picked you up earlier tonight to take you to the water so you could drown yourself. Remember? But instead I took advantage of the situation, which was a shitty thing to do, I admit, but since I'm a sociopath, as officially diagnosed when I was just a kid, long before I got promoted to what I am now, I can't say I care much. Basically I raped and killed you. You wanted to die, anyway, so I figured what the hell, it was kismet. But you got away before I could finish. So here we are."

"I don't understand…"

"It was a shock to the system. You had a temporary memory lapse. That often happens during the transition. It will all come back to you, though. I mean everything, before we even met this evening until this very moment. In fact, you're still in the process of turning. Sometimes it takes a while. Everyone's different. Depends on your constitution and your acceptance of the inevitable. I thought I was doing you a favor, actually. I mean, I would've done it anyway, because that's what I do. But it seemed like the solution was obvious. So I did what I did then you escaped and ran off and this is how it worked out. Like I said, kismet. Without even planning it I solved all your problems, and mine, too. At least for tonight. And even in eternity, that's all you ever really got. Some things never change."

The woman felt a chilling spasm of deep dread. "Are you saying what I think you're saying?"

The cabbie finally turned and faced her directly. An abrupt, conveniently timed flash of bright lightning illuminated his ugly face and sharp fangs. Horrified, the woman watched her own reflection in his rear view mirror slowly then suddenly vanish.

"Now I'll never die," she whispered to herself as the truth dawned on her and it began to rain outside.

"Well, there are ways," he said. "There are always ways, if you really wanna go there. Immorality, or I mean, immortality ain't for everyone, it seems. So there are options. None pretty. All pretty grisly, in fact, which is why even the nutcases like you typically decide to just say fuck it and move on and make the best of a vastly improved situation."

"Options? To this? Like what?"

"You really wanna know? I mean, you still wanna follow through on how and why we first met to begin with?"

"I do. More than ever."

"Really? I'd think whatever was bothering you before would be cured by now."

"No. It's worse. Because now I remember. Everything. I wanted to die exactly because of men like you."

The cabbie laughed. "Men like me?"

"Not exactly like you. Just the evil part."

The cabbie nodded and sighed. "That cloud cover is deceiving. It will be light soon. We need to wrap this up. Now you can either go back with me to the station and sleep it off, so to speak, or we can just end it all as you originally requested. I kinda feel responsible now, honestly. I ain't all bad, see."

"Help me, please."

"Okay. Let's go someplace quiet first."

The cabbie drove her into a remote, wooded area as "Love You So"—the lyrics promising eternal amorous rapture—played continuously, like a broken jukebox. He stopped and got out and went to the trunk. Then he opened the rear door and helped her out. He was brandishing a blood-stained axe.

"Is that the only way?" she asked, trembling in the cold storm, though it wasn't the source of her chill.

"Yep. Then I'll bury the pieces separately - so they won't reconnect."

"Promise?"

He smiled, again revealing his drooling fangs. "You can trust me."

THE LOST SOCK

Everything you do feels like an act of desperation. Even something as simple as doing your laundry.

First you have your morning coffee, even though it's just after midnight. You've lost all concept of time since you lost your day job and gave up your saxophone lessons. Again. You like your coffee "Barack," as opposed to "Michelle." Your ex-girlfriend, a heavily tattooed punk-goth chick who had a Tura Satana body to go with her Bettie Page haircut, or maybe it was the other way around, gave you a lot of crap for putting so much cream in your coffee, since she preferred her coffee like she preferred her men— strong, and dark. What she ever saw in you, you'll never know. Eventually she dumped you for an African athlete. Irony is so funny, except when the joke's on you.

You want to believe good things happen to good people. You want to believe hard work always pays off. You want to believe the universe is ultimately benevolent, that someone up there is looking out for you, as long as you look out for yourself. You don't want to think that Life is either totally random, or calculatingly cruel. But you find it increasingly difficult to even get out of bed in the morning, because of so little evidence in support of this basic effort. It looks like you'll be scraping the bucket until you finally kick it.

Doors are closing all around you. You feel trapped, suffocating. You wonder what's the point. Of anything.

And yet you still decide to do your laundry. You need further pointless distraction from your distress. This turns out to be your biggest mistake ever, even though as usual, you are not to blame. Or so you keep telling yourself.

When the hell was that zombie apocalypse supposed to kick off, anyway? It seemed way overdue, and it would solve so many of your (and the world's) problems by leveling the survivalist stakes for everyone on the planet at once. Death was the great equalizer, after all. But zombies are like private jetpacks. Another broken promise for a fabled, fabricated future already diminishing in the dust of your delusional dreams.

You leave your dark little semen-smelling room and head down to the laundromat, the one next to the all-night diner. Normally you like to sit there moping over pie and coffee while you pretend to read the newspaper or a paperback crime novel, like a character in an Edward Hopper painting, but you can't even afford that right now. You are always lost inside your own head. It is scary in there. The only place scarier than the space inside your skull is the vast wasteland outside of it. This is why you prefer your relatively less frightening internal world. It's smaller, more manageable. You can lose yourself inside of it, without losing anything else in there, not even your mind.

Or so you thought.

You jog through the light rain to the laundromat with your bag on your back like a Sad Sack Santa, stuff all your cheapjack, thrift-store bought clothes into the washing machine, and pop in the requisite quarters. You don't separate the colors from the whites because you are strongly against segregation. You fancy yourself a bleeding heart liberal, but that's only because your heart is broken and leaky. It really has nothing to do with compassion for your fellow human beings. You can relate to their struggles and squalor, but only offer synthesized sympathy from a safe distance. The truth is you don't separate your laundry because you are too cheap and lazy. Meanwhile, you blithely detach yourself from the rest of humanity.

The place is very sterile and antiseptic and brightly lit, like a Chinese restaurant or cafeteria, and there are no other people around at this late hour sharing in your solitary sartorial sterilization. The laundromat is open 24 hours a day, seven days a week, even on holidays. It is run by people who don't care about religious observances or national celebrations of historic milestones and patriotic valor. They just want their god damn money. You can understand that bottom line philosophy. Clothes get dirty every single day. Filth never vacations. The owners of the laundromat, whoever they are, are providing a valuable service. Unlike you. You've never done anything for anybody your entire life. You are a self-centered schmuck. But with a sparkling wardrobe. It's the least you can do. If you can't help anyone else, or even yourself, you might as well not offend anyone's sense of sight or smell. This way you're practically invisible. Nobody notices you. Nobody cares about you. And the feeling is mutual.

You sit there staring into space while listening to the music playing softly over a mysterious sound system. Oddly, it's the old Tom Waits album "Rain Dogs." One of your favorites. It crackles and pops like a well-worn LP. Better than the painfully bland Muzak you typically have to suffer through. You wonder if you're actually listening to the secret soundtrack of your own tormented spirit, psychically emanating from the outdated jukebox of your own time-battered brain, which is finally drowning out your sonic surroundings. You check to see if you're wearing earphones for your iPod. Then you remember you don't own an iPod. Could never afford it. You do have an obsolete laptop at home, but you can't afford Internet either, so it's basically worthless. Like you. An archaic relic from a bygone era. You need to be donated or recycled or simply destroyed. And yet you keep barely functioning, because if you didn't do your laundry, who would?

After the first wash cycle, you break out of your daze and remove the vintage copy of *American Splendor* from your back pocket and begin reading or at least looking at the illustrated, mundane misadventures of your spiritual brother, Harvey Pekar. Harvey is dead now, probably in a happier place, which would be anywhere but Cleveland. You've read this particular issue dozens of times. Harvey's love for jazz and comics resonates with your own personal tastes, but your connection goes much deeper. You're both so lonely. At least Harvey eventually found his soul mate, Joyce, and even adopted a daughter. A movie was made about his life and self-made career. Even though he never quit his day job as a file clerk, he died relatively successful. You should be so lucky. Right now you don't even have a job, not even a shitty one. You're rationing out your change for laundry, which is essential for basic existence. Soon you'd run out of coins altogether, then where would you'd be? Same place you've always been: nowhere.

You move on to your beat-up Black Sparrow edition of Charles Bukowski's *Ham on Rye,* another book you've read repeatedly. You carry it around everywhere you go—which is hardly ever much further than the corner cafe—and read it obsessively. Bukowski is another writer who magically made a lucrative career out of being a drunken bum. What was his secret? Luck, you surmise. Just plain, dumb luck. Talent, too, but a lot of people have that. Luck is a much rarer commodity. You drink a lot too, even if it's potato vodka out of a plastic bottle lately. Maybe you should drink more. Yea, that's it. It's all coming clear now.

You put your clothes into the dryer, and keep reading, or least looking at the pages filled with words that describe your own situation, but with a hardboiled, poetic eloquence you will never achieve. Someone else, someone duly famous, has to express your pathetic little anonymous soul for you. That's part of the problem. You have no artistic outlet, no creative skills, no way to sublimate or vent your frustrations, not even on the World Wide Web, like so many of your fellow malcontents, furiously trolling through various sites, firing off bitter insults to complete strangers, pumping up their own self-esteem by gleefully undermining others'. You would if you could, but you can't, so you don't. You have nothing.

Except a batch of clean clothes, which you begin taking out of the dryer and placing on the counter so you can organize them before stuffing them back into the bag, which was also washed, so it's all wrinkled, but it stretches out nicely as it's filled with warm duds.

You go through your clothes piece by piece, folding them neatly, placing them each individually into the bag, and then you realize you're missing a single sock. A black sock. The one you masturbated into just a few hours ago while watching a Raquel Welch movie. Since the sock is black, the semen stains would show, but because you knew you were about to do a load of laundry after you shot your load anyway, you simply tossed the soiled sock in with the rest of the clothes, without even rinsing it first in the sink. For a sense of completion, you chucked its barely-dirty companion in with it, and left the house sock-free, loafers only, a la *Miami Vice*, not wishing to "ruin" a perfectly good pair, since you preferred returning home with a full set of clean clothes after your weekly sojourn, so you could start your life over again all fresh, over and over. In fact you are only wearing an old Devo T-shirt and a pair of shorts despite the wet, chilly weather, and those were direct from the "clean" drawer and could be worn for another day or so, starting your new, endless cycle of dirtying, then cleaning. It was a system that gave your life some semblance of sense. You had it all perfectly planned.

Except for this part. You can't just lose a sock. Especially one possibly stained with evidence of your lonesome perversion. Sometimes the semen, especially when freshly applied before the inevitable machine washing, requires giving the sock a second rinsing in the sink back in your room, and then you can hang it out to dry on the windowsill. You can't ever open the window too far anyway, or else your cat will escape. Your cat is your only friend in the world. And your precious prisoner. She's also the only remnant of your most recently failed relationship, with a human female, that is. So your place is perpetually dank and stuffy because you can never open the window too far. At least it's cold outside now, with a brisk winter breeze wafting through the crack, so you don't need to open it too far anyway, and it's a comfortable temperature in your room, at least not until spring. Thank God for the little things that make life worth living, if only barely like the relative relief of regular seasons. No matter what, the world is constantly changing around you, even if you yourself feel totally stagnant. Time will eventually cure your sense of stasis. There's always tomorrow, right?

But first, you need to find that sock, or else all is lost, not just the sock.

Looking back, you realize you should've used a paper towel or toilet paper, but you're trying to conserve those, since you can only use tissue of any sort once, whereas a sock is relatively durable. Upon further regrettable reflection, you deduce you should've at least jerked off into a white sock. But you were randomly flipping channels on your pathetic little portable semi-color TV, and after briefly pausing on the latest ghoulish news report about a local serial killer suddenly there's Raquel Welch in all her youthful glory as a scantily-clad cave-girl, and you wanted to seize the moment, along with your already stiff boner, so you just grabbed the sock off your left foot and did your business. You didn't want to soil the sheets because that would require possibly a second load to wash, and you are too low on quarters to accommodate such an extraneous expense. The shooting semen had to be carefully contained. You really should've at least rinsed it off first. That was stupid and impulsive. At least you didn't wipe your ass with it. But that might be next, if you don't find a job soon.

Frantically, you go back through your entire batch of clothes, item by item, wondering if the sock was static clinging to your underwear or a dish towel or something. You hang tightly onto the single black sock—which is definitely not the one you used to clean the cum off your drained, withered cock and hairy balls and pasty thighs, since it was the one with the tiny hole in the big toe part, making it easy to distinguish, and disqualifying it as an impromptu jerk-off rag. You didn't want any semen seeping through the hole back onto your fingers, perpetuating the cycle.

Speaking of cycles, you stick your head deep inside the dryer, feeling out every nook and cranny of the still-warm interior, practically tearing the filter into pieces. You have a distinct memory of putting that semen-covered sock into your dirty clothes bag. That was an undeniable, indisputable fact. That sock was definitely not left behind in the house. It just had to be somewhere in the immediate vicinity.

But it's not here, and it's not there. It's not fucking anywhere. It simply vanished into seemingly thin air. But how the hell is that even possible, given the basic laws of physics and nature and the whole god damn motherfucking universe? You're not a science geek by any stretch, you're a high school dropout, for Chrissake, but this simple deduction didn't require a diploma, much less a PhD in Physics or even Theology. How can something of physical dimension suddenly disappear without a trace? That just wasn't possible. It defied simple logic and reason. There had to be a solution, an explanation, otherwise life itself made no sense. And if life is senseless, what's the point of living it? That missing sock held the key to everything missing in your own life. Somehow, you know this. Or so you choose to believe. Faith is always a matter of choice.

Your panic spiking to the point you nearly faint, you begin desperately combing through every other washer and dryer in the joint, even though you have no memory of putting any stray articles of clothing in any other machine, but you have to look everywhere. And you do. Inside the machines. Beneath them. All around the floor. In every corner. The sock is simply nowhere to be found. Its companion is as lonely as you are now. And likewise perforated and vulnerable. Without its perfect match, it has lost its reason for existence, or as the French fancily phrase it, its *raison d'etre*. Just like you. You feel strangely bonded with that lone sock. And for once, regardless of your lifelong, self-imposed isolation, with everyone in the entire world. Finally, you all have something crucial in common.

You grab your bag, the single sock still clutched in your grasp so it could perhaps attract its long-lost mate like a magnet or track it like a bloodhound, and head back out into the dark, stormy night. It is pouring now, making your search that much more difficult, but, praying you dropped the sock on your way to the laundromat so it never even wound up in the washer or the dryer, you backtrack your steps carefully, peering into every gutter, every sidewalk crack, up and down every alleyway, sopping wet from tears and raindrops, lightning flashing and thunder booming all around you. It is a waking nightmare.

Despondent beyond endurance, you finally return to your little room, sans the missing sock. You lie on your bed and gently weep as your cat lies next to you, purring, trying to comfort you in your misery, as is her custom. You reach down and gently pet her. Then you get up and feed her, just to show your appreciation for her feminine if feline company. You also open the nearly empty fridge to idly feed yourself as well, but you're not hungry anyway, so you slam it shut. It's the middle of the night. Outside the storm is still raging. Life feels so incomplete with that sock. You thought your life sucked before, but at least way back then, only two short hours before, you still had all your clothes. Unlike the rest of your sad little world, your wardrobe was intact. The one complete thing in your life. You figure you could always go out and buy another pair of socks once you found another job. But what about the poor sock left behind? You couldn't just mix 'n' match. That would be unfair to the abandoned sock. You had to find its missing mate. This was your new mission in life. If only you could find that sock, you'd feel complete again. Lonely, unemployed—but with all your socks in matching pairs. All of them. No one could ever take that away from you. Until now.

You can't lie down and relax, much less sleep. You're a night person anyway. You pace the creaky floor, your mind racing down the road to nowhere. Your stomach is tied in knots, churning with inconsolable grief. You can always find another girlfriend. She obviously wasn't your perfect match. But this sock only had one mate. They were literally made for each other. You just have to find it, for its sake, and for yours. For everyone's. You have to get to the bottom of this. You would finally solve this universal riddle afflicting millions of people throughout history, or at least since the invention of electric washers and dryers, which was the source of the problem, anyway. So much for technology, that sucker-punching scourge of self-destructive humanity. You would find your lost sock, and all the lost socks, and become an international hero for the ages. Your ex-girlfriend would beg you to take her back, and you'd just...well, consider it, anyway. She did have a great body, after all. But this is beyond personal acclaim and empty fame. This is a quest for the Ultimate Solution to the Mystery of the Universe. This is why you were born, you tell yourself. Finally, your sorry little life has a purpose.

Let it go, a voice inside you says. But you ignore it. You've listened to your inner voice before, and it only got you into trouble. That's how you met your previous girlfriend, and all of them. This time it feels somehow different, more like an alarm than an admonition. But you ignore it anyway. You're blinded and deafened by obsession. You promise your cat you'll be right back. She stares back at you with a strange sadness, as if she knows something you don't, but she often looks at you this way. You ignore her profoundly melancholy expression, even as it tears at your heart.

Despite the deluge, you rush out into the storm still wearing only your Devo T-shirt and shorts and head back down to the laundromat. This time, it isn't empty. Not completely. There is a sole woman sitting in a green, plastic mid-century modernist chair, wearing nothing but a long, shiny, black leather raincoat, and black pumps through which her red-painted toes show elegantly and erotically. No socks for her to lose. Smart. She may have clothes beneath the coat, but judging by her bulging cleavage, it doesn't seem like it. They may even be inside the washer, as you don't notice a laundry basket nearby. You wonder what her story is. Why is she cleaning her clothes at this time of night? Someone that stunningly beautiful can't be lonely. And why did her clothes require an emergency cleansing? Defiantly, she is casually dragging on a cigarette right beneath the NO SMOKING sign. She is also wearing dark sunglasses. Though to be fair, it is pretty bright in there. For all these reasons, you find her immediately mesmerizing.

Momentarily distracted by lust, you stand and stare at the mystery woman for a moment. Suddenly she turns her head and returns your gaze. Since you can't see through her dark shades you can't make direct eye contact, but you feel her looking right at you, right through you, and you shudder, not from the cold night air which extends into the heat-free laundromat, but from acute self-consciousness. You put your head down and walk back to the dryer to give it one more search.

But it's currently in use by somebody else. Someone else's load is whirling around inside that dryer, your dryer, obscuring the object of your desire, the goal of your journey, not just tonight's routine if fateful trip, but stretching back to your birth on Earth. It all came down to this very moment. Instinctively, you know this to be true. Or so you keep hoping.

You politely ask the woman if she is using this particular dryer. She nods slowly in the affirmative.

This is so fucked, you think. What are the odds that someone would be using your dryer in an otherwise empty laundromat filled with perhaps twenty dryers, along with twenty washers? The odds are good if the Universe hates you, you surmise.

But wait—maybe the missing sock wasn't even left behind in the dryer. Maybe it was still stuck to the inside of the washer. In your hyperventilating haste, you hadn't even checked there! You open it up and grope around the cold, metallic sides of the washer, filled with renewed hope. But your hopes are quickly dashed as your hands come up empty.

You sit back down with your head buried in your hands.

"Lost a sock?" the effortlessly seductive woman asks suddenly, in a cold, flat tone, which still sounds sexy given her naturally silky voice.

You perk up like an aroused puppy tempted by a tasty treat. "Yes!" you say with measured optimism. "How did you know?"

"Happens all the time," she says with a sigh. "Lost socks. Lost keys. Lost pets. Lost opportunities. Lost loves. Lost people. Where the hell do they all go?"

"You got me," you say with a shrug. "The world is a finite place, after all. Maybe another dimension?"

"I think I can help you," she says simply. "There is one place you haven't even looked."

"Really?" you say, hope renewed once again, but cautiously.

"Yes." She stands up, walks over to you, and opens her raincoat. She is indeed naked beneath the coat. Spectacularly naked. Other than the raincoat, she is wearing only her pumps and her shades. Her hair is long and red and thick, her skin a creamy alabaster and totally unblemished, her erect breasts perfectly pointed, her vagina...right in front of your face.

"Here," she says. "Reach inside there."

"Where?" you whisper in dumbfounded awe.

"There." Further exposing her magnificently curvaceous torso and luscious loins by spreading the thick leather coat with her expertly manicured, red-painted fingertips, she steps even closer, so her well-coiffed, sweet-smelling pussy hair is brushing up against the tip of your shivering nose.

Reluctantly, you put your two right forefingers into her hot, moist vagina and feel around meekly. Though tight-lipped, the squishy chasm feels like it goes on forever.

"Deeper," the mystery woman moans as her head falls backward.

You feel suddenly paralyzed with belated shyness. "Um...."

"Deeper," she demands sharply. "It's in there. Trust me. Find it."

Compelled by her carnal command, you force your entire hand into her vagina and rummage around while the woman begins to writhe with orgiastic pleasure. As she screams in climax you slowly remove something long and soft and dark, soaked in vaginal juices, but unmistakably your missing sock.

You're so ecstatic and excited you get a boner that begins leaking visibly through your shorts.

"You have to wash those now," the woman says.

"N-now?" you stammer.

"Yes," she says, kneeling before you and unbuttoning your shorts, pulling them down around your ankles. She then takes your penis in her mouth and swallows you whole.

You cannot believe your good fortune. Your head rolls back, heavy with sheer bliss. After an audible gulp, the woman wipes the residue of your semen off her gorgeous full lips and licks her long, slender fingers, like your cat does to her whiskers and claws after devouring a meal composed of dead, canned flesh. You see the woman—whose stomach ironically is now as full of your semen as your lost sock was—smiling slyly as you bring your head back up following your delirious orgasm. She is no longer wearing her sunglasses as she stares right through your skin and deep into your soul. Her eyes seem to be glowing neon red, burning holes in your hazy brain, but everything suddenly feels so surreal, you can't be sure the delectably demonic vision isn't being filtered through your own warped imagination. Stuff like this just doesn't happen every day. Not to you, anyway.

Then the woman suddenly grabs the sock from your limp grasp, swiftly ties it securely around your neck, and begins rapidly tightening it like a noose.

You are definitely not imagining this.

You can't breathe. You can barely even see. It's all a gradually fading blur. Your tongue begins dangling out of your drooling mouth. Your eyes tear up and begin bulging out of your blushing face. You begin vainly kicking outward and flailing your arms in protest but she is very tall and strong and easily overpowers you.

You feel her kiss you once deeply on your gasping mouth as if sucking out your final breath before she leans over and whispers in your ear, "Now you will finally find out where all lost souls go..."

You black out. Not temporarily. Forever.

Deep within the Dark Void, you finally find the Final Answer. To Everything. But you can't even share It, because you're gone now, totally incommunicado with anyone alive. Everyone here will have to find It for themselves. The hard way. No posthumous glory for you.

The official cops' report claims a janitor discovered the body of a middle-aged male at the laundromat early that morning, apparently a victim of self-asphyxiation with his own sock while shamelessly masturbating in a public place.

Meantime, your cat is back in your room, crying for you. Eventually she pushes through the barely open window crack and is soon lost and alone in the cold, cruel world. And there's nothing you can do about it. It was just a soulless sock, you idiot.

Thanks for the snack, by the way. See you in Hell.

NIGHTMARE CLOUD

Life for the lonely man had become like a dream when the dreamer realizes it's a dream, so nothing seemed to matter because none of it would last, because none of it was real. He felt like he was slowly disappearing, as if he'd never existed, like he could just vanish in a puff of smoke and nobody would care except his cat, and even the cat would find a way to move on fairly quickly. So he did what he always did when steeped in self-loathing and suicidal depression: he went to sleep. And he slept and he slept so he could dream and dream some more.

That's when he met Her. She had an hourglass figure he wanted to make time with.

In the dream, a song he was only vaguely familiar with called "I'm Only Happy When It Rains" by a band called Garbage was playing as She danced a striptease in a storm. The wind whipped Her dress up, exposing Her beautiful body, but he was primarily entranced by Her mesmerizing otherworldliness. She was visually alien to him, and yet he felt he knew Her, a distant memory magically manifested, much like the song She was dancing to so gracefully and sensually, Her bare feet splashing puddles, the flimsy dress sticking to Her figure, revealing only the shadowy, sensuous contours. They were in an alleyway between two old brick buildings, the type Seattle was losing rapidly. This gave the scene a timeless aura, like an Edward Hopper painting.

He was so fearful he'd never see Her again that he

could barely enjoy the present moment. He was always this way. He felt if something couldn't be documented, it didn't actually happen, even if the moment was mundane and not worth recording. It still mattered to him, because one is only allotted so many moments in this life.

Immediately and instinctively he pulled out his smartphone to film this sensuous spectacle, like it was a spontaneously produced music video. At one point he had aspired to become a professional photographer, taking pictures of Nature and architecture that interested him, but like all of his professional daydreams, it died a painful, premature death. Only his somnambulistic seances were providing him any true satisfaction.

He took some snapshots first, basically action stills, wiping the raindrops off the screen as he went, and then tried taking a video. But just like that, She vanished. The rain dried up, the sun came out, blinding him like an interrogation lamp, and he was suddenly drenched in sweat in-stead of rain.

He woke up wet. The alarm on his phone was going off. It was the same song from the dream, "I'm Only Happy When It Rains." He didn't remember setting that song to wake him up. He hadn't downloaded it on purpose. In fact, the only tunes currently on his phone he deliberately stored there were from the Billie Eilish album *When We Fall Asleep, Where Do We Go?*, as well as the Spencer Day album *The Mystery of You*, both for their melodic melancholia and depressive romanticism. He'd already burned out on Chris Isaak and Duffy. He remembered hearing "I'm Only Happy When It Rains" on the radio a few times years ago, but never really thought about it much because though the lyrics were ironically sad, the tempo was too upbeat. Now he was obsessed with it. Repeatedly, he scrolled through the songs downloaded on his phone, but couldn't locate it. It was gone, like the mystery girl in the wet dream.

Out of desperation, he also carefully checked the photos and videos on his phone, but She wasn't there, either. He'd left his dream phone behind, in the dream. If only he could've backed up the evidence here in the waking world, to prove She actually existed, somewhere, somehow, whoever She was.

He sat in the Lost Lake Lounge in Capitol Hill, staring at *Night of the Living Dead* playing silently on the TV with closed captions. He drank two Manhattans. Then he headed over to the Cha Cha Lounge, below Bimbo's Cantina, and drank two Margaritas while gazing at the burlesque performance film *Teaserama* featuring Bettie Page, Tempest Storm, Lili St. Cyr and other dancers of the era, also playing silently as the young hipsters barely glanced at it, laughing with condescension. Feeling his age and his isolation from society, he looked around at the comforting *lucha libra* iconography and velvet paintings of masked Mexican wresters and nudes and tropical scenery, illuminated by strings of Christmas lights. Then his eyes met with those of Laura Palmer from *Twin Peaks,* depicted in a velvet painting above a booth where two young girls were giggling and talking. The sadness overwhelmed him. He walked back to his apartment nearby to sleep, even though it was only 10pm. But that's when the crowds of clones poured in, which only made him feel lonelier.

When he lived in Tacoma with his ex-girlfriend, they often went out drinking together. After she suddenly left him one day, leaving only a cold note containing little in the way of explanation beyond simple ennui, he went out nightly to their favorite places, like the popular tiki bar Devil's Reef, and of course the Zodiac Supper Club. But the memories of them together soon overwhelmed him. It wasn't sweet sentimentality. It was self-suffocation. He had to leave town, but not go so far he'd forget her entirely since his memories of her were all that sustained him, even if he was in constant pain. He feared the only other alternative. So he moved north, relocating to the Seattle branch of the boring company that reluctantly employed him. He wanted to quit, but he needed the money to live, and the only reason he wanted to live was so he could remember his ex-girlfriend. But now she had been replaced by Her, and all he wanted to do was escape to the dream, and for that alone, he needed to survive this miserable little life for as long as possible.

But a rendezvous inside a revery is not an appointment that can always be kept.

He became so worried he wouldn't see Her again he had trouble falling asleep. Plus he was consuming too much alcohol, which made him both drowsy and restless. Popping two Xanax, which he scored secretly without prescription, he remained rigid for a while before he suddenly relaxed and he was finally, blissfully unconscious.

She was there, dancing in the alley as it rained. But this time the music was a hedonistically hot yet carnally cool baritone jazz saxophone, and She wore a tight bustier, nylons and high heels, like the long dead ghost dancers in *Teaserama*. He reached into his pocket for the phone so he could take more pictures and video. There had to be a way to capture and preserve Her, if only virtually. His memories of Her were not reliable, murky at best. Even now, confronted by Her directly, Her facial features were both gorgeous and ill-defined, like a fresh painting getting pelted with raindrops. There needed to be a record of Her existence outside of his subconsciousness, if only for his sake. He needed proof he was not totally alone. After a few snaps and some live footage, he woke up, and she was gone.

He checked the camera roll on his phone anyway. Just pictures of the *lucha libra* images from the Cha Cha Lounge, along with Bettie Page and friends. That happened, he knew for sure, since it was a memory he could revisit in the temporal plane, but they themselves weren't real. Not anymore, anyway. The dancing woman in his dream was real, at least inside of his head. He could still feel Her, even if he hadn't affirmed Her tangibility yet. Even now, Her presence resonated in his psyche. If he closed his eyes, he could see Her, but not touch Her. Only himself.

After yet another daily waking wet dream, he popped some Xanax and fell into a deep sleep, and there She was, taunting him with Her elusive beauty. Only this time, she was completely nude, dancing to music he'd never heard before. It was like mixtape of Tangerine Dream, Jean-Michel Jarre, and Johnny Jewel. She lured him into Her arms, and they embraced as it rained. There were only silhouettes of tall city buildings in the distance, shadowy outlines of factories spewing white smoke into the gray skies, but no discernible structures to distract them. It was like they were making love inside of an abstract painting by Salvador Dali. He came inside of Her, again and again, kissing Her neck and breasts as She laughed and cried, whether from pain or pleasure or both.

After She lay beneath him, with both of their sexual juices leaking copiously out of Her vagina, blending with the puddles of rain, creating psychedelic streaks like oil leaking into a stream, he reached in his pocket for his phone, but then realized he was naked, too. He'd entered the dream sans any clothes or recording devices. As She began to dissolve into the colorful cocktail of rainwater and bodily fluids, he tried to grab and hold Her, but it was too late. Like his buckets of semen, she merged in liquid form with the flowing rainwater, and washed away down the neon-lit street.

He woke up wetter than when he had fallen asleep. His sheets were soaked with his semen and perhaps other fluids. He reached for his phone. Desperate, he checked his photo roll anyway.

There was a series of images depicting the area where they had made love, the rain and the buildings, which were fully visible in high definition. The river of rainwater rushing down the neon-lit street was there, too. But She wasn't. Maybe he had only imagined Her, even in his dreams.

Still, the fact that these images had somehow been captured and saved to his real-world phone meant he had psychically broken the barrier between consciousness and subconsciousness. He couldn't stop staring at them, insecure in their veracity since perhaps he had snapped them while awake and forgotten them, but their eerie similarity to the nocturnal visages haunting his thunderstruck head was unmistakable.

It was another dark, rainy day in Seattle, and his workday went by quickly, as if he were still dreaming. Maybe he was. But since he could feel and smell and experience his ambient surroundings, it didn't matter to him. The people around him were merely phantoms, anyway, even before he met Her.

Just for the sake of confirming his own sanity, he finally did ask one of his co-workers whether he saw the photos on his camera roll, showing them off with pride.

"Yes," the co-worker affirmed.

"Do you recognize this place?"

"No."

"Good." With that outside, unbiased corroboration, he now felt suitably vindicated. His apathetic co-worker had no personal agenda to discredit his cognizance, so why would he lie? Clearly, his dreams were more than delusions, since their documentation was now accepted in the corporeal realm.

When he wasn't at work, he was alone watching his favorite movies at home, like those by Jim Jarmusch, which were always about loners and outsiders and misfits, or offbeat horror films from all eras such as *Daughter of Horror* (1955) and *Under the Skin* (2014), his increasingly ignored cat by his side, lost in the alternate realities as created by others much more successful than he in this rewardless endeavor called Life. That's all he ever did since She came into being. He never went out drinking alone anymore, because it was too unsatisfying, so he settled for junk snacks washed down by plastic bottles of vodka. His health was rapidly declining, but he was no longer concerned with mundane self-maintenance, much less the emotionally remote company of fellow sentient beings. No one alive or dead could compete with Her elusive presence now constantly permeating all of his senses. The world around him had lost all appeal, all meaning. He merely slept-walked through his daily routine, killing time working and watching movies and drinking, so he could finally go to sleep and be with Her.

That night, he was back in the *Blade Runner*esque dreamscape, but She wasn't there. He had his phone with him, and took pictures of the deserted urban shadow-world, more an artistic reflection of Seattle than its exact duplicate.

John Carpenter-styled synth music (or at least that's how it sounded to him) began playing all around him as if performed by a celestial orchestra, and suddenly She was there, wearing a flowing black gown, much like Valerie Leon in *Blood from the Mummy's Tomb* (1971). In fact, She looked a lot like that actress, at least in her current iteration. He attributed this to the fact he had just fallen asleep watching that film on television, and the music to the fact he had recently watched John Carpenter's *Prince of Darkness* (1987) as well. Before this, as noted, Her facial features were always somewhat vague, contorted within the confines of his rainswept field of vision, but now they seemed more clearly defined as She approached him, arms outstretched, Her bosoms gradually revealed as the straps of the black gown fell around Her shoulders, Her long black hair billowing in the breeze like a thick, wet, wobbly frame around her glowing, ivory face.

But first he had to take a picture of Her. As he did, She laughed and laughed. Then She vanished and he woke up.

Checking his phone, he saw Her. She was merely an outline in the rain, her contours recognizable if not clearly defined, but at least now he had evidence of Her existence outside the dream, or at least of a true entity whose identity was not merely a product of his fevered imagination, born of a lifetime of loneliness.

For weeks and then months on end, or so it seemed, She visited him nightly and they drowned in rapturous, rain-soaked sex, his camera roll now loaded with proof, as if he needed anyone else to believe him now. He only needed to convince himself, and that had been accomplished. The more pictures he took and saved to his phone, the more clearly Her features became defined, along with their surroundings. Oddly, when he was awake, the opposite was happening. He felt like he was dreaming while at work. Even the old brick buildings of his Capitol Hill neighborhood began to assume the qualities of a three-dimensional oil painting. His co-workers began gradually then completely vanishing. Finally, only one was left. And even his features were sketchy and out of focus, as if peering from the other side of a fishbowl, his face now like an unfinished sculpture.

The dreamer asked his co-worker, "Where is everybody?"

"Who is everybody?"

"The people who were here."

"It's just us. It always was. You must've imagined the others."

"Look at these pictures on my phone. What do you

see?"

"I see nothing. It says you're out of storage space. There are no photos. Maybe you deleted them by accident. I hope you backed them up."

He checked his phone and indeed, that was the warning. No more storage space. All of his photos had also vanished. He could only hope they had been backed up somewhere accessible, if momentarily elusive. Technology was not his forte. This is why he had such a lousy, low-paying job, sitting in a cubicle surrounded by strangers, now reduced to a single shadow.

"Would you like to go out for a drink?" the dreamer asked his co-worker. Suddenly, he was lonely, so lonely he couldn't wait for sleep to rescue him from reality.

"I have to do my laundry tonight. Sorry."

He never saw his co-worker again. The next day, he was all alone at work, as well as at home. Instead of horror or Jim Jarmusch movies, he watched old *Ren & Stimpy* cartoons, hoping some outlandish levity would boost his spirits. But he did not even see Her in his dream that night. The following morning he was in a total panic, constantly checking his phone, but the pictures were all gone. They had been uploaded to his brain, which was impermanent and unreliable, easily hacked by his own mortality.

Two more nights went by, and she remained out of frame. The third night, he was so anxious, he did not sleep at all. On the way home from work the following day, he picked up some sleeping pills, since not even the Xanax was calming his nerves enough to sleep now.

Then that night, after swallowing the pills, he saw Her again, more grateful than ever for Her existence even if it was ephemeral and undocumented. Their lovemaking was so intense that he forgot about the pictures. They rolled around in the rain, fucking and cumming and fucking and cumming more and more and more, as if this was their endless fate. It was only afterward, as they lay together exhausted in a stream of rainwater and semen and vaginal juices, that he remembered.

"My pictures all disappeared from my phone," he told Her. "Even the ones I took while awake. I'm out of storage space."

"That means it's time," She said.

"Time for what?"

"Time to end all time."

"But this is only a dream."

"This is not the dream."

Abruptly, Her flesh began peeling away and dripping like bloody, fatty meat down a slaughter-house drain, running off Her in a rush as the rain cleansed her bones, leaving a thin layer of translucent skin and a wet, wind-whipped mane of silver hair framing Her grinning skull. Only Her piercing emerald eyes, gelatinous, purple vein-laced pale breasts, and gaping vagina remained intact, all oozing blood which dripped down Her seductive, cadaverous figure in sanguinary torrents.

As his very essence withered in horror, She took his phone from his violently shaking hand and showed him a series of photos which he had never seen. "*This was the dream,*" she said in a hissed whisper. There were pictures of him in his cubicle at work, then lying in his own bed, masturbating while watching television, blended back to back into one monotonous mosaic. Finally all the pictures were of him just lying in bed, staring at the television with his limp dick in his hand. Then his eyes were closed in many pictures, all in a row, as if it were a flip-book chronicling his unconsciousness, when he was no doubt here, with Her, at least in his mind. She kept scrolling and the only detail in the remaining photos that constantly changed was the light in the room. His face remained still, his body remained prone. The tone of his skin gradually morphed from white to blue. Because, he finally understood, he had died in his sleep, having inadvertently overdosed on the sleeping pills. He only hoped his cat wouldn't starve to death, but then she showed him pictures of the cat leaping onto the bed and eating his eyeballs out of their sockets and chewing his fingers and devouring his penis. Nobody came to look for him. Nobody missed him. His body would rot in isolated oblivion, at least until a bill collector knocked on his door and noticed the horrible stench. He was out of their reach, at least. Now he only existed within this dream of an eternity with Her.

She laughed and she laughed and he fell to his knees, holding his head in his hands, covering his ears, but he could never, ever block out the eternal echo of evil emanating from his skeletal soul-mate.

As they made violent love, and his Eternal Lover's clawed, bony hands raked the flesh off of his quivering torso and screaming face, he imagined Her the way She had been, when he was still living in the world that now only existed in his own fading photographic memory.

DEAD NUDES

The stripper parked directly in front of the club where she danced. If Luck was a lady, then she was wet and ready for entry. But Luck was taking the night off.

The Little Darlings strip club was located on Westlake Avenue in downtown Seattle, across the street from the retro-futuristic eyesore of the Amazon Spheres. The club's adjacent store, Fantasy Unlimited, catered to all manners of sexual pleasures and perversions, the types of products you couldn't order online. She'd never once gone inside, either the porn shop or the Amazon complex, as if there was a true distinction. The architectural and cultural contrast and ironic proximity of the two supposedly disparate businesses never really registered in her social conscience, or what was left of it. Commerce and commodities didn't interest her, other than those that directly benefited her own survival. She was there to work, to make money, not spend it, at least not on this junk. She was running late so she quickly went straight to the dressing room to get changed so she could undress again to the go-go beat of her professional theme song, "Hush," by Deep Purple. It was always her intro, even if the audience was small, as it was this evening. It was eerily deserted. In fact, there was only one customer, sitting at a remote table, not even paying attention to her or to anything, it seemed, just staring off into an unseen abyss. She hadn't noticed any other girls in the dressing room, either. She was all alone with the stranger.

After she came out wearing nothing but her pasties, G-string, and high heels, she walked over to the booth where the DJ usually was. But nobody was there. She looked at the old-school 1950s stardust clock on the wall, which she hadn't even noticed before. It read 8pm, exactly her normal start time. So she wasn't late. She was right on time, as usual. She prided herself on both her punctuality and her perky breasts, which were organically perfect.

Then "Hush" began playing, right on cue, as if by dark magic, and instinctively, she climbed up on the stage and reluctantly began her routine, solely for the benefit of the single stranger. He was sipping a radiant cocktail that glowed in the dark like radioactive waste, but the bartender was not in sight, either. She wondered if the stranger had gone behind the bar and made it him-self.

The stranger wore an overcoat and a floppy hat. His hands were visible, looking leathery and liver-spotted in the dim light, but his face was hidden in shadow. He creeped her out, but since she had already punched in, she figured she might as well just keep dancing.

"Hush" ended, replaced by an unfamiliar melody. It sounded like vintage burlesque jazz music, the kind her father, a cabbie, listened to on the radio all the time as she rode around in his backseat. She never knew her mother growing up, but later in life, tracked her down in a strip club in New Orleans. After her mother had been knocked up, she stuck around long enough to spit out a daughter, then split with no forwarding address. Her father never recovered, eventually succumbing to pulmonary edema, or at least that's what she was told. She came home from work one day and found him dead, drowned in his own fluids. Or someone's.

But the stripper eventually bonded with her mother, who was once a Playboy model as well, she later discovered through her own research. Otherwise, her mother's life was largely a mystery, so the daughter became her own detective. In fact, one of the customers who frequented Little Darlings was an ex-private eye. Now he was just a dog walker nursing a broken heart. They had a fling because he reminded her of her dead father. The ex-private eye was dead inside, too. Later, her mother seduced the ex-private eye, and mother and daughter became estranged once again. It wasn't that the stripper was in love with the dog-walking ex-private eye. It was because she knew her mother only did it to prove she still had it, that she was the dominant female in the family, and could have—or leave—any man she chose, even one dating her daughter.

The mother moved away again after spending some time with her daughter in Seattle for their brief reunion. The stripper continued in her line of work because it paid more than waitressing, the only other job she felt qualified for. She hated being in the service industry, which was why her time as a prostitute didn't last long, either. As a dancer, she felt more in command of her own stage in life. Dancing—a designation she preferred to "stripping"—was her calling. She also belonged to a burlesque troupe that performed around the Pacific Northwest, called the Betties, after Bettie Page. The stripper and her female friends—who were more like casual acquaintances, since she never truly connected with anyone—sometimes went drinking together at the Cha Cha Lounge in Capitol Hill, where the old burlesque film *Teaserama* played silently in a constant loop on a big screen in the far corner of the bar. The stripper often imagined herself in that world. She idolized Tempest Storm and Bettie Page and Lili St. Cyr. They were performance artists, like her. Except they were legends, immortalized on film, and she was nobody, damned to oblivion.

Only famous people had names all the anonymous people recognized and remembered. The ex-private eye turned dog walker had pointed that out to her, and she agreed.

Once she told him he objectified the female form. "You call it objectification," he said. "I call it worship." She agreed with this, too. Eventually it ended anyway, as all things do.

She occasionally dated customers after her fling with the ex-private eye went sour, and slept with the manager sometimes with no strings attached, but basically she kept to herself, living alone with her little dog, the only person that understood her and cured her loneliness. That's how she met the ex-private eye turned dog walker. She didn't miss him, because she still had her dog. Her neighbor, a lonely old man, looked out for the little dog now and then, in exchange for an occasional blowjob. It was worth it. She needed to save her cash for retirement.

Even though the music selection was unusual, she went with it, since it reminded her of her burlesque act. Typically management wouldn't permit such nostalgic indulgence, since it wouldn't appeal to their demographics. But apparently she had the place all to herself tonight, except for the stranger. She was used to being alone. It was the aching loneliness that killed her daily. She knew the difference.

The big screen TV behind the bar flickered on, and it beamed images of fires, floods, and other disasters, natural and man-made, like wars raging everywhere, for no good reason. Again, there was no one behind the scenes pushing any buttons. This reality TV programming just happened by itself, unprompted. She wondered why they were showing the news, which was always depressing. People came here to escape the outside world, at least when the place was packed, not dark and nearly empty, like now. But the music kept playing, and so she kept dancing, without exhaustion. She looked at the spikey Atomic Age clock on the wall. It still said 8:00. Unless she had been dancing for twelve hours straight, it was broken. The scenes of chaos and horror continued unabated on the TV, with only two pairs of eyes for an audience, and not even they were interested. The lone stranger didn't move, just continued staring at nothing, not even her, and sipping his drink, which never depleted.

Finally, she had company.

She was joined on stage by a dozen other dancers, all nude except for high heels, but their expressions were vacant as they swirled around her. They reminded her of a movie she saw once with the ex-private eye, his suggestion, called *The Incredibly Strange Creatures Who Stopped Living and Became Mixed-Up Zombies* (1963). She stopped, though the music continued. She recognized one of them as her mother, when she was young, her age, in fact. The other dancers—including Bettie, Tempest, and Lili, among other unfamiliar faces—were unresponsive, their eyes cold and dead, staring blankly into the dark distance even as they mechanically moved in time with the music. Feeling unsettled surrounded by these curvaceous zombies, she left the stage and sat down with the stranger.

He looked up and revealed a face both ancient and timeless. It was free of wrinkles, yet grizzled. He was bald and his eyes were gray. The bones of his face were sharp and almost cut through his thin flesh. She felt a chill as he looked into her eyes. She knew who he was, and suddenly, where she was.

"Why am I here?" she asked him. "It's not my time yet."

"There is no time here," he said.

It was true. She felt frozen while also in motion. Nothing around her changed except for the other dancers. The TV images, the clock, the stranger, the music. It all combined to produce an effect of serene stagnation. Oddly, she felt no fear. Not yet.

"You're safe in here with me," he said to her. "Just look." He gestured toward the end of the world being televised. "I'm not who you think I am. I'm not your enemy. I'm your greatest friend. Your savior."

"What do you want from me?"

"I want to feel something."

"I bet you do."

"Yes, that too. But it's more than that. I desire true intimacy, however transitory, for it can be transcendent."

"You want to have sex with me?"

"I want to worship your living vessel. Normally I come to ravage and destroy your kind. But I am weary. I want to experience the joys and pleasures of the flesh that I ultimately consume and digest and expunge like so much worthless waste."

"I don't know that I want to fuck Death."

"I will fuck you eventually."

"Are you saying you'll let me go if I do this with you, voluntarily, right now?"

"Nobody escapes me. But I can offer you comfortable sanctuary, as opposed to the alternative."

"Which is?"

"You don't want to know. Ever."

"Why choose me?"

"I've been watching you, but then I watch everyone, everywhere, biding my time, until it's their time. *Our* time."

"That doesn't answer my question. Why *me*. Here. Now. *This*."

"It's rather arbitrary, though your youth and beauty are universal in their representation of sexual desire. But as for why you and not someone like you, it's simply because you were the first to walk in that door. I was already here. But then I'm already everywhere. This is how it works. It's not always a plan. It's often just a random selection. The opportunities present themselves, and I take advantage of convenient vulnerability. I don't create these circumstances. I merely bring them to their logical conclusions, at least per my rationale. Everything ends the same way eventually. The only difference is the timing."

"But then where is everyone else?"

"Out there, where you definitely do not want to be. The horror of what you call Life is engulfing the Earth. The virus known as humanity is finally being expunged by Nature herself, doing much of my dirty work for me. This leaves me with some time to kill."

"So who are these other dancers? And why is my young mother one of them?"

"They're not real, not like you and me right here and now. They're shadows of their former selves, visualized echoes of an ephemeral existence that only feels eternal in the moment, but that's part of the illusion. This is all a background show for your benefit. The entire world, in fact. Even the music."

"That's not really my style, old man. And I don't find the television programming very entertaining, either."

"That's so you know and understand that this is the only place in the Universe where you're safe, at least for now."

"So say that I fuck you, or let you fuck me. What then?"

"You will have to do more than merely submit. You will have to please me."

"I can do that. But what's in it for me? You're not really my type, so it's not like I'll enjoy it. You're basically asking me to hook, which I've done before, but out of desperation, and for a price. I turned those tricks to pay bills. What's the pay-off here?"

"You will remain here forever."

"With you?"

"Yes. You will be my bride until the end of Time, which has no end."

"That sounds boring as Hell. Literally."

"You won't be bored. You'll have whatever you please. This will be your private oasis."

"Look, if you can conjure these perfect women behind me, why not just fuck *them*? Why do you need *me*?"

He leaned over and placed his bony hand on her face, then shoulder, then breasts, and whispered through his dripping saliva, "Because I want real flesh, not masturbatory fantasies."

Repelled by the cold touch of his fingers, she sat back and considered her options, looking up at the televised apocalypse, then around at the familiarity of the club, which was relatively harmonious.

"Can I bring my dog?" she asked after some contemplation. "He's my only friend in this world. And the next."

"Yes," he said. "After."

"One more thing," she said.

"Yes?"

"If I please you, if it's everything you hoped it would be and more, I get to choose my own fate while still alive. Then later, you can have me."

He considered it as his gray eyes beheld her body, then he nodded in the affirmative.

"Okay," she said. "Let's do this. Where?"

The light around them changed to a purple, twilight glow, the stage became a massive, plush bed with a pink spotlight, isolating it within a void of impenetrable blackness.

"I think this will set the mood," he said as he removed his clothes. Jeff Buckley's cover of Leonard Cohen's "Hallelujah" permeated the chamber.

"That's my favorite song," she whispered. "I always want to use it for my closing routine, but management never lets me, because it's too slow and sad."

"I know. You're under new management now, as it were. This is your closing routine."

Fighting back tears induced by the song if not the situation, she walked over to the bed and lay down on the luxurious mattress, seductively removing her pasties and G-string and high heels. He removed his coat and hat. His body was gaunt and pale and covered with lesions. But his veiny erection was massive. She achieved multiple orgasms as soon as he entered her, filling her warm body with his vile fluids. He suckled her breasts as she moaned and bucked beneath the savage thrust of his insatiable lust for the embodiment of Life.

This went on for hours or days, possibly weeks, then years.

Finally, he was fully sated. He rolled off of her and didn't move. At all. He was depleted, exhausted. Death was dead. Gradually, then quickly, he disintegrated into dust.

At the same time, in a slow cinematic dissolve, the world around her reverted to normal, or least the normalcy she once knew and now cherished more than ever. "Hush" was playing, and she was dancing on stage to a packed house. The drinks were flowing, the customers were happy. The TV was showing episodes of the old *Playboy After Dark* TV show, on which her mother had often appeared. She recognized her on the screen, and felt proud. All was forgotten and forgiven now. Around her there was vitality and Life, amid all the misery and horror, balanced as it should be.

She still felt all alone, but at least she was finally free.

That night she went home to her little dog, her best and only friend, if only for a little while, and hugged him with renewed appreciation for his brief existence.

She was overcome with joy and relief at her own reprieve, lying in bed listening to Jeff Buckley's "Hallelujah" on repeat, fully aware of the ghastly specter peering at her from outside the window, floating in mid-air completely unseen by mortal eyes, weeping at the loss of his love whom he could never touch again because she was forever beyond his reach.

MOOD MASSACRE

"Fuck you and the whore you rode in on," she told him just before she shot his dick off. It was already a hell of a honeymoon.

"Nobody is born perfect," he moaned with agony as he rolled around in his own blood, desperately trying to reattach his mutilated member.

She kissed the gun barrel and said, "Nobody dies perfect, either."

She always knew how to spoil a mood. This was the first time she'd killed one, though. And she wasn't about to stop here. She looked and behaved like a deadly dominatrix from an Eric Stanton illustration or a Russ Meyer movie. On purpose, since these were two of her lifelong reference points and sources of aesthetic inspiration. These larger-than-life qualities, both physical and attitudinal, were what had initially attracted her husband. Late husband.

The bellboy down the hall had heard the shot, and without even knocking, he unlocked the door and walked in to see the blood-splattered bride in all her voluptuous, gory glory, wearing nothing but her late husband's brains, a flimsy powder blue see-through nightgown that barely extended down to her upper thighs, her pink high-heeled fluffy bedtime slippers, and her tattoos of Native American symbols that only she could decipher. Except for fellow Native Americans, of course. She was only part Native American, though. The rest was a mix of Spanish and Italian ancestry. She was naturally hot-blooded, a walking combustible cocktail of feminine fury, finally unleashed.

"Well, whaddya know," she said with a lascivious sneer as she sized up the unwelcome party crasher. "The bellhop's tears really keep flowin'. This must be the place. You ever been to Graceland, kid?"

"What?"

"You know, the palace of The King. In Memphis, Tennessee."

"N-no."

"Well, then it's time you met Elvis, isn't it?"

Naturally conflicted by the lurid spectacle, the bellboy froze in place as the bride approached him, set down her gun, knelt before him, pulled down his pants, and began to perform fellatio on his limp, quivering penis. He was internally aroused but externally paralyzed. She knew just what to do. Sticking the forefinger and middle finger of her right hand up his anus, she suckled his testicles until his erection was firm and leaking. As soon as she put it in her mouth, he gushed a load down her throat. While he was dizzy from the sudden sex attack, she gulped down his essence, wiped her mouth and licked her lips, picked up the gun, stuck it up the crack of his ass, and pulled the trigger.

Leaving the bellboy writhing and screaming in a billowing pool of his own blood and semen, the bride left the hotel room, walked down the hall past a terrified couple whom she ignored, and pushed the down button on the elevator. She felt like she was in a trance, imbued with a mysterious, malevolent force of vengeful Nature.

When the door opened, there was a lone, lonely,

ugly, misshapen, middle-aged man, standing rigid, both horrified and mesmerized by the horrifically erotic apparition. She walked in and the doors automatically closed behind her. By the time they opened again at lobby level, the ugly man was dead on the floor of the elevator, his pants around his ankles, his guts pouring out of his punctured posterior.

After flinging off her gore-soaked nightie, the bloody bride strutted through the lobby, gun and breasts pointed outward, thwarting any attempts to stop her, though the desk clerk was dialing 911. His stammering explanation of the reason for the call made little sense, giving her plenty of time to exit onto the street, past the astonished doorman, who actually held it open for her. Last time he'd seen her, a few hours earlier, her groom was carrying her inside. Apparently she was experiencing buyer's regret.

It was a brisk, cool, dark evening in the downtown section of the seaside village. Autumn leaves blew beneath her heels as she continued up the street, avoiding eye contact with the astonished passersby. Sirens wailed behind her, their lights flashing blue and red onto the orange shadows and purple twilight bathing her stark, savagely sensuous silhouette.

When the police car screeched to a halt on the sidewalk in front of her, she was kneeling before a dirty, homeless hippie sitting on a bench on the edge of a quaint little park. As soon as the hippie came in her mouth, she stood up, spit it back in his face, stuck the gun in his mouth, and said, "Now swallow this." The cops were too late to stop her from demolishing his skull, but they were shouting demands for her to drop her weapon. However, as she swerved toward them, gun outstretched, brain-splattered breasts swaying, they hesitated a second too long. She blew both of them away with twin head shots, then walked over their prone bodies and continued down the suddenly deserted main street, with no particular destination or agenda in mind. She felt hypnotized by her own rage as she continued her random rampage, targeting only males, since they were susceptible to her seductive appearance despite any other inhibitions or concerns regarding their own safety. Before she shot them, she seduced them, with minimal effort required. A quick moment of carnal pleasure with the likes of her was apparently worth the cost of their lives. She was amazed at how much semen she swallowed in exchange for the souls of lustful, desperate, stupid men. She hated them all, even as their fluids dripped from her lips and down her body, blending with their blood. She was sticky with liquid male essence. A shower would be required at some point. After she felt finished.

Finally, she was out of bullets, which meant no more blowjobs, since there was no trade-off for her. She'd had her fill, anyway, and her point had been made. She didn't fully comprehend why all the men immediately acquiesced to this grisly, pornographic *quid pro quo*, other than men are simply stupid, and then they die with a stupid smile on their stupid faces.

She walked into a little bar and sat on a stool, dripping numerous bodily fluids, and said to the male bartender, "Can I get a shot of bourbon to wash down all this cum and blood?"

Nodding nervously, the man poured a shot, and left the bottle. She'd laid her empty gun on the bar, so he didn't reach for the phone. Like the few other patrons sitting there staring at her in awe, he was frozen with fear, shock, and desire.

"I'm ready for a gin Martini now," she said. "I'm celebrating my wedding night."

"Neat or on the rocks?"

"Up, like you are right now, but with olives instead of stinky, shrinky old man balls."

"Coming right up."

"Yeah, I bet."

She selected songs by some her favorite singers, including Julie London, Billie Holiday, Ella Fitzgerald, Sarah Vaughan, and June Christy, then sat back down to her perfectly chilled Martini, which she sipped slowly. There were no sirens in the distance. She'd already killed the two local cops on active duty. Most people within eye and earshot had shuttered their windows and locked their doors to keep the female monster out of their homes.

None of the men in the town had any intention of turning her in, anyway. She was just too good to be true.

This stalemate went on for about an hour, quietly except for the songs on the jukebox.

Behind the bar, the bloody bride noticed a machete was displayed, above the bottles glowing in the backlight, next to the velvet painting of Elvis Presley.

"Is that thing real?" she asked the bartender.

"Yes. It belonged to my grandfather. Took it off an enemy in the war. He killed gooks with it."

"Which war?"

"All of them."

"Can I feel it?"

"The machete?"

"Yes, what else?"

"It's pretty sharp."

"Good. I'm counting on it."

The bartender pulled out a stepping ladder, climbed up, reached high, and removed the machete from its mount. She stood up when he handed it to her so she could fully appreciate its lethal majesty, suggestively stroking its sharp blade, slightly slicing the tip of her right forefinger, then sucking her own blood while licking her wet lips. Next, still carrying her cocktail in one hand and the machete in the other, she went over to the silent jukebox, set her drink down on top of it, then went about carefully choosing more appropriate mood music for the impending occasion, including Bauhaus, The Cramps, Sisters of Mercy, the B-52s, Blondie, Devo, Billy Idol, The Talking Heads, and Joan Jett, ready to really rock now. She admired the eclectic selections, especially impressive for such a small bar in such a small town. It's like it had been curated just for her, just for this moment.

"Okay, any ladies in the house, please leave now. Sorry, but I don't swing that way. Not since college, anyway. Plus I don't want any of you to get hurt." But the women had already fled. Only the men had stayed behind, over their companions' protests. The men came in all colors. But they only had one flavor. They all tasted the same to her, like juicy flabs of stupid meat.

The bride walked over to the pool table, cleared it of any round or otherwise obtrusive objects, then demanded each man lay on top of it after removing their trousers, one by one. Immediately they formed a single file line, stroking their dicks to achieve maximum readiness.

"All right, calm down, fellas," she said dryly to the anxious men, downing the rest of her drink then snapping her fingers at the bartender for a refill. One by one, she rode each one until reaching mutual satisfaction, then chopped their heads off—both of them, above and below the waist— causally taking sips of the fresh Martini carefully balanced on the pool table's edge in between sessions. None of the victims declined or protested, happily accepting their fates, turning their backs on everything they had supposedly held sacred, including their loved ones, in exchange for intimacy with this enrapturing goddess of pleasure and pain.

Once she was filled with the fruitless semen of every man in the room except the bartender, she returned to her stool, sat down, and ordered yet another gin Martini. He had it ready in a jiffy, though he looked worried.

"Then what?" he said. "I mean, after this?"

"Maybe one more for the road. Then I'm leaving. I've done everyone I can do here."

"That's it?"

"Yeah, what did you expect?"

"Well, what about me?"

"What about you?"

"Isn't it my turn?"

"For what?"

"You know…like them."

She sighed and said, "I'm feeling pretty full and sore, but all right. So make it good, old man, because it's the last drink you'll ever make." The old man grinned while popping a pill for his erectile dysfunction. Soon his ancient, withered tool was up and running.

Ten minutes later, the bloody bride left the bar full of drained, decapitated, emasculated corpses and continued up the dark, windy road, her heels clicking ominously on the wet pavement, the gore-drenched machete in one hand, her to-go Martini in the other.

As she thoughtfully sipped her cocktail, burning out the bitter aftertaste of semen and souls, tottering a bit from the combined intoxication of the booze, orgasms, and slaughter, she thought about her stepfather, who had repeatedly molested her as a teenager. She had pleaded with him to stop, finally threatening him, but he wouldn't, so she put rat poison in his wine and that was that. Her mother didn't even ask any questions. She'd told the cops it was suicide. In a way, it was. He'd been repeatedly warned, after all. But even knowing the consequences, he refused to stop. Because that's how most men are. They either don't believe the threat of obliteration, or else they just don't care. They'd rather die than deny their own base desires, however perverse, immoral and transitory.

Then eventually the bloody bride met her husband, who had once been quite the playboy. He was also a filmmaker who made dirty underground "art films." In fact, that's how they met, when she auditioned for one, and she earned not only the starring role in the movie, but in his life. Even though she knew his reputation as an unrepentant ladies' man, that he'd always had a straying eye and a wandering penis, she trusted him, but with a non-negotiable caveat she hoped and prayed he'd take seriously, since she did love him. She warned him if he ever cheated on her following their engagement, she'd kill him. Completely enthralled with her curvaceous, Amazonian beauty, he eagerly agreed. Then on their wedding night, worried about maintaining a life of strictly imposed monogamy, he impulsively and drunkenly banged one of the comely bridesmaids (also one of his actresses, who was likewise in love with him), performing the rushed act of betrayal in their own honeymoon suite when the oblivious bride went out to pick up some more champagne.

After she returned sooner than expected and caught them in the act, she mercifully let the remorseful bridesmaid go after pistol-whipping her with the gun she'd secretly packed in her suitcase, a gun which, ironically on purpose, had once belonged to her late stepfather. She knew it would come in handy one day, for similarly vengeful reasons. Her groom had been warned, just like her stepfather had been, but tragically, like all weak men, the groom apparently decided the surreptitiously enacted illicit sex was worth the ultimate price of his own life. It had been his call, foolish as it was, and she had no pity for him. He had left her no other choice. The penalty for infidelity was death. But for him, perhaps it wasn't punishment. Maybe in his primitive brain, it was a totally fair trade-off. One moment of fleeting forbidden pleasure in exchange for an eternity in the dark dirt. He must've thought it was worth it, otherwise why make that choice? She'd never know for sure, but it didn't matter, anyway.

In that moment, the bride realized all men, at least straight men, would gladly die for sex with a beautiful woman, like her. So she obliged them. She had loved her groom, and she'd always liked men, despite her stepfather's abuse, but only for one thing. That's all they were good for, since that's all they really wanted. Then they were immediately disposable. She felt complete empathy for the black widow spider. She understood the insects' instincts now. But it was time for her to die, too. Her mission would never be complete, anyway, until all men were wiped out. It was an impossible task for one woman to accomplish all by herself. She would need a globalized army committing mass, simultaneous insurrection against their patriarchal masters. But then not all men deserved it. She felt sick with guilt and exhilarated with catharsis at the same time. In any case, for purely practical if not moral reasons, it was time to end this carnal carnage. She was ready to reunite with her husband, if only so she could laugh in his stupid skull face as it blazed forever in Hell.

Since she really needed a bath anyway, she walked slowly into the sea, trance-like, letting her machete drift away along with her soul, until she heard the voice of a man, a fucking *man*, yelling from the bow of a yacht floating nearby, just off-shore, about to embark on an epic journey of celebratory debauchery.

The mournful, murderous mermaid was rescued against her will and dragged aboard. She knew if she were a man, especially a black man, they probably would've just her drown. But she was too good to waste. This was one reason why she immediately resented them. Her theory was proven just as quickly.

One of the eager, youthful male passengers, who claimed to be a medical student, took her to his cabin and gave her mouth to mouth resuscitation, holding onto her bare breasts for lecherous leverage. It did not end well for him. She began French kissing him, he quickly removed his clothes, she bit his tongue off, and then she performed fellatio on him after stuffing a blood-soaked sock in his screaming mouth. Then she bit off his penis and spit it out, and he fainted from shock and loss of blood. Next she went up on deck and looked around. The boat were out at sea, though the shore was still in sight. This ship had already sailed, in all senses.

She ran into the sole female passenger, a hired stripper/prostitute, who was wearing a bikini and high heels and a sad expression of professional resignation.

"Are you part of the party?" the hired stripper/prostitute asked. "I thought I was working solo for this gig."

"What's the gig?"

The stripper/prostitute explained. Apparently the yacht belonged to the President of the United States, a brash, middle-aged, handsome billionaire who ran as an Independent and bought his place in history. His college-aged son, who was about to be married, was the current captain of this boat. It was a floating bachelor party, with a tacky tiki theme, and the boys were already stoned, sporting cheap, red fez hats and smoking jackets with nothing underneath but young, horny bodies. They were ripe for the fatal orgy about to ensue.

"You need to get on a lifeboat and leave," admonished the bride. "Now. For your own safety. They plan to repeatedly gang rape you, and you won't be able to report it because of their connections. In fact, they'll probably just toss you overboard like so much trash in the middle of the ocean when they're through with you. But don't worry now. I'm working undercover. There's going to be a raid. Coast guard, police, FBI, Miami Fucking Vice. Leave. *Now*."

"But what about my little dog?"

"Take him with you. He may get hurt in the crossfire."

"Okay. I hate these creeps anyway."

The bride helped her and her little dog escape. The other healthy, young, male passengers were up front, oblivious in their revelry, not even noticing one of them had been missing for some time.

Wandering around the cabin undetected, the bride discovered some expensive assault rifles locked in a glass cabinet in one of the rooms. This was going to be fun. Then she found the music collection, removed the Les Baxter album from the turntable, and instead put on the LP soundtrack for Rob Zombie's *House of 1000 Corpses,* which blared from the intercom. Not that she considered it a point of merciful redemption, but they had good taste in music and women, at least. Guns, too. She selected and slung one of the sophisticated military-grade weapons over her shoulder, holding another with the other hand, then walked up to the deck, where all the dancing drunks turned and gaped at her as she began to writhe with sinister sensuality in all her nude majesty, hoisting both guns in the air. Then they smiled and laughed and whooped, thinking this was a surprise from the host's wealthy, powerful father. The bride smiled, too. It was already over. Next stop: the White House. Since only men were in charge there, nobody would stop her from cleaning up the mess they had made of her life, and so many others like her. She may eventually die a martyr, but at least it was for a good cause. And she'd be immortalized as a symbol of feminine sexual liberation.

Meantime, all she had to do was set the right mood.

SLAUGHTER OF THE SENSES

The naked bodies of her dead lovers were buried in the basement of her callous conscience. But so what? They didn't deserve her anyway, much less their own lives.

Of course, she lived in an old brick apartment building in the Green Lake District of Seattle, and she had no actual basement, not to call her own, anyway. There was just a laundry room, which of course couldn't cleanse her soiled soul. But in her mind, they were all there, the rotting corpses of her past, haunting her night and day as she went about her business, which was nobody's business but her own.

She had a recurring nightmare or perhaps just a nocturnal vision that she had single-handedly slaughtered every last man on Earth after fucking them, sometimes *while* fucking them. It was probably inspired by something she read somewhere. It wasn't a political statement against patriarchy. It was simply an expression of her own primeval urges, left unchecked in the depths of her depraved imagination. She had multiple orgasms as she masturbated to the scenarios swimming around her subconsciousness like piranhas in a vast, thick pool of bodily fluids.

Her day job was tending bar at the Shanghai Room nearby in Greenwood. Sometimes she hopped over to the adjacent North Star Diner and took orders behind the counter. But she preferred the amber coziness of the bar, which was lined with wood-paneling, Christmas lights, and several screens on which she often played the original Universal monster classics, along with Hammer horror films, without sound as the exotic music of Martin Denny, Les Baxter and Arthur Lyman or sometimes goth surf music by Messer Chups or psychobilly by The Cramps played over the sound system, putting a smile on her pretty face as she slung out the signature North Star cocktail and the Shanghai Sling in copious amounts, like a leaking, alcoholic vagina. She was obsessed with horror movies, hard booze, and no-strings sex with strangers. This was why she often seduced male and female customers and took them home with her, never seeing them again. Not because she killed them. She just grew bored easily.

In fact, she was becoming so accustomed to this routine that she was beginning to lose interest in anything corporeal. She was barely forty years old and looked at least ten years younger, just approaching her sexual peak. But instead of an insatiable appetite for the pleasures of the flesh, her one-night stands were quickly becoming exercises in tedium, repeated as a matter of rote routine rather than a deliciously cathartic release of pent-up passion.

She'd never been married or even engaged, endured four abortions going back to her teens, and even had a serious boyfriend once. He was gone now. She never talks or even thinks about it. It was a sticky subject. But then sex is always a sticky subject, she figured, at least if you do it right.

A co-worker at the diner suggested the bartender was suffering from depression. They had sex once, but then the bartender dumped her. They still got along, despite the lingering one-sided sexual tension, since the bartender didn't feel any pressure. It was just the waitress, who was pressing for a three-way, if only as a way to get back into bed with the emotionally elusive bartender.

"I don't feel anything," the bartender said as she dragged on a cigarette out back during a break. The waitress was also on break. It was the middle of a gloomy, soggy night, and very slow. The establishment was open 24 hours a day, making a mockery of time itself, like the nearby Snoqualmie Casino, where they once went to gamble, drink and fuck.

"I went through the same thing till I started taking antidepressants," the waitress said. She was also pretty, much younger, twenty-five or so.

"And?"

"Now I feel sad at least."

"Never happy."

"Sometimes I remember happiness."

"Same here. I don't need prescription drugs for that."

"But do you ever feel sad?"

"Never."

"It's a sad world without any tears."

"It's a sad world anyway. That's why I smoke, drink and fuck so much. To forget this is all a dream. Might as well make it a wet one."

"I can make you happy if you let me. At least for a little while."

The bartender touched her cheek, and wiped away a tear. "You did. But that was that. No need to get bogged down and entangled and attached. I'm already bored with everything. If I get bored with you, then it's over."

"What is?"

"You and me. *This*. Everything."

"What if we bring someone else into it for spice?"

"Another woman?"

"A man."

"Who?"

"There's a guy sitting at the counter right now. He's just your type."

"Which is?"

"Lonely."

"That's basically everybody or anybody if they're being honest."

"Exactly."

The bartender considered the proposition, along with her profound sense of ennui, which had descended on her suddenly, engulfing her completely, rendering her barely functional, as if someone had dropped a barrel of black oil on her, soiling her spirit while paralyzing her desire for anything, even death.

Finally she responded, "If we fuck him, can we kill him afterwards?"

The waitress smiled and shrugged nonchalantly. "Sure."

"Okay."

The waitress assumed the bartender was kidding.

They both were working the swing shift, and got off at 3am. They were both ready to get off again right after that.

A rare thunderstorm had commenced, and rapid lightning flashes illuminated their dark scheme as they tossed their cigarettes onto the wet pavement in tandem with an abrupt downpour. The flash storm augmented the already auspicious atmosphere.

The lone man had moved from the diner to the bar,

awaiting service. He was wearing an over-coat over a nice suit. He was handsome and solemn. They wondered why he had no date, but then it was quite late. Perhaps he had ditched him or her already. In any case, he was moving on from coffee to cocktails, so obviously he wasn't calling it a night just yet.

"What'll it be?"

"The usual," he said.

"You're a regular? I've never seen you before."

"But I've seen you. Many times."

The waitress brought his fried cauliflower wings from next door and set them in front of him. She returned to the diner after winking at the bartender. A few kids, high on dope and life, had come in to order a very early breakfast.

"I'm assuming you mean the North Star, since that's our house drink."

The lone man nodded. "That's it. See? You know me after all."

"I know what you like, anyway."

"You do. I've been watching you. You know what everybody likes."

The waitress got an ominous chill, and it wasn't from the breeze wafting in the open backdoor, which they had forgotten to close. She looked at the clock. 2:15. In 45 minutes the relief shift came in, and she and the waitress could go home. She was thinking maybe without this guy, though. He was hot but creepy, like those fake vegan wings.

Dracula (1931) was being displayed on the surrounding screens silently as Robert Drasnin's exotica album *Voodoo* played in the background for aural ambience. The man was wordless and motionless, lost inside his own head. Finally the bartender grew restless and made her move, the same move she always made, because it always worked.

An hour later all three were in her big, brass bed inside her brick-ensconced apartment, a Jess Franco movie playing with the sound low on her big screen TV. She left the window open so the lightning, thunder and wind could complement the natural and unnatural and supernatural sexual forces being unleashed within the bedroom. The candles she lit were immediately blown out, but the electrifying storm illuminated their bodies enough for unbridled carnal navigation.

The lone man furiously fucked and came inside every suitably accessible orifice of both women, who consumed his copious bursts of semen with voracious thirst. They likewise came multiple times, their own juices coating their thighs, which they licked off of each other as they ate each other out while the lone man masturbated and came in a geyser all over them, providing them with even more organic liquid sustenance to lap. The scent of flesh and fluids soaked the already dirty sheets and filled the dank air.

Afterward, the bartender lay perfectly prone, casually smoking a cigarette as the lone man and the waitress slept. The Jess Franco movie had ended, so the TV screen was blank, like the world inside her head. After staring at the whirling ceiling fan for an hour, she finally drifted off as well. The storm had likewise subsided. All was calm, at least on the outside.

When she woke up, the man was straddling her with a switchblade to her throat. Beside her, the waitress lay still, her eyes wide open, staring at nothing forever. Blood was still gushing from her savaged throat, covering her pointy, perky breasts in a sweet crimson sauce, her nipples still erect like little cherries on two scoops of melting vanilla ice cream. The bartender thought she looked like an erotic sundae. Then the lone man grabbed the bartender's face and refocused her gaze on her own impending fate.

"You shouldn't have let me in," he said as he pressed the blade against the bartender's throat.

"You shouldn't have come in," she said with her eyes glowing neon red as she lifted both feet upward and entwined her calves around the man's head, jerking him backward in a single thrust. She said, "Time to meet Elvis. Let's not keep him waiting." Then she grabbed the blade from his unsteady hand and pinned him down on the lower end of the big bed. Their situations had reversed too quickly for him to adequately respond. She rode atop his exhausted penis until it was hard again, and when it was, she inserted it into her wet vagina and slid down, holding the blade to his throat as she hungrily kissed his mouth and face and muscular arms and chest. When she felt him tremble with orgasmic release, she jabbed the knife repeatedly into his neck. His blood splattered all over her entire torso as she came, twice.

Next she licked the blood off his neck and chest and likewise the bucket's worth of blood off of the waitress's body, her tongue like a brush creating an abstract oil painting on a canvas of dead but still warm flesh. She heard a masculine murmur of pain and realized the lone man was still barely alive, so she sucked him erect again and he gurgled his final bloody breath in perfect tandem with his final ejaculation, which she mostly swallowed, the massive load of semen spilling out of her lips as she gagged, dripping down her chin and blending with the blood on her large but firm breasts. It felt as if she had literally sucked the life out of him, and she smiled with a strange satisfaction.

Arising from her bed of horrors, the bartender walked across the room and stood in the window, her blood-and-semen drenched body silhouetted in the moonlight like the perfect portrait of primal passion. For the first time in a long time, she felt truly alive. But that sensation was already slipping away, along with the transient beauty of this singularly wonderful night.

She then flopped down between them and gradually fell asleep, awaking hours later to the stench of grisly sex and rotting corpses, reminding her of the cinema of Lucio Fulci, her favorite filmmaker next to David Cronenberg, David Lynch, Jean Rollin and of course, Jess Franco. She'd always been a freak, which scared off many of her suitors, despite her sensual allure. Recently she had seen Fabio Frizzi preform his original score for *The Beyond* (1981) live at the Fremont Abbey, and she smiled at the memory, which now blended with millions of other images in her brain like a dollop of paint in an expressionistic painting, forever still yet seemingly moving, if imperceptibly.

Wearily, she got up, went to the kitchen, made some coffee, smoked another cigarette, put on a West Coast jazz compilation album, cooked and ate an omelette, then took a butcher knife and began messily chopping the bodies into pieces, which she then placed into several plastic bags. The gore seeped through so it would be obvious to any potential onlookers she wasn't merely doing a little spring cleaning. After all, it was late autumn. She'd probably take a shower soon anyway, she figured. Not yet, though. She was enjoying the full sensory immersion in utter perversion too immensely at the moment. Like everything else, it too would pass, so she tried to squeeze as much pleasure out of it as possible.

It was her day off so she had time to just sit and listen to West Coast jazz all day, wondering what to do with these body parts. Chet Baker, Dave Brubeck, Art Pepper, Stan Getz, Chico Hamilton, Paul Desmond, Stan Kenton, Gerry Mulligan. Then she remembered that while the building did not have a basement, it did have a laundry room. So at least she could bleach her sheets. It was while she was down there that she got the idea of dicing the bodies even further and simply putting them piece by piece into the garbage disposal. It would take a while, but she had time. She wasn't due back at work until the following evening. She'd probably have to cover the waitress's shift as well, performing double duty. That was fine with her. She liked being productive. Keeping busy helped her forget how bored she was. She still felt nothing inside. Nothing at all. She was dead beneath her skin, and had been for some time. Too long to care about anyone or anything. When fatal ennui consumed one's conscience, empathy was always the last thing to go, at least for those who had it in the first place.

The problem with trying to force pieces of the bodies into the garbage disposal was that she could only strip off the flesh and chop up the guts and viscera, some of which she cooked and ate out of gruesome curiosity. The bones would clog and fuck it all up. But bags of bones would be simpler to conceal.

Once the skeletal remains had been bleached, she wrapped them in some old blankets she'd been meaning to get rid of anyway, including the ones stained with the semen of the dead man, and took them down to her car.

She drove deep into Snoqualmie and buried the bones and blankets deep in the darkly emerald forest. Then she treated herself to lunch in the restaurant at the Salish Lodge, AKA The Great Northern, one of her favorite spots, in a window seat overlooking the famous falls, sipping her favorite cocktail, at least that she didn't make, called "The Dale Cooper." The soundtrack to *Twin Peaks: The Return* played in her head, and she was momentarily content. Then suddenly, or so it seemed, the contentment was over.

That night at work everyone was in a panic when they realized the waitress had not shown up for duty, and had in fact disappeared. The police arrived, asked questions, looked around. The bartender had not shown up for work, either, so they went to her apartment. She was in bed smoking a cigarette and drinking a Vesper as she watching David Lynch's *Lost Highway* (1997), casually considering her options, annoyed by the rude intrusion. The cops had made the decision regarding her fate for her, apparently.

"You were the last person seen with her," one of the cops said to the bartender.

"Yes, she came home with me and another man after our shift."

"What man?"

"Didn't catch his name. We all slept together, then they both left. That's the last I saw of them."

The police were skeptical, and asked if they could

examine her apartment, without a warrant, which they could obtain anyway, but they wanted to get this over with, since there were many other mysteries to solve, like the secret of Life. She agreed. She had nothing better to do.

They found blood stains on the hardwood floor, which in her haste she'd neglected. They would've been a bitch to clean, anyway. She was handcuffed without protest and taken down to the local precinct and booked on suspicion of murder. But then she simply confessed, telling them about the buried bones. The male victim turned out to be a notorious serial killer. The waitress also had a secret, violent past, since she was the serial killer's half-sister, thought to be estranged since childhood after an incestuous upbringing which often included four-ways with their stepmother and uncle, who was later arrested for killing his brother, their natural father. Apparently the two semi-siblings had recently reunited after being separated for years, and eventually became accomplices in a string of sexual murders. Ironically, the police found the remains of their victims not far from where their own had been buried by the bartender.

"I only killed the dude," she told the interrogators.

"Who killed the sister?"

"I guess he did. I woke up and found her dead, and then he tried to kill me, so I did him first. Self defense."

"That's not how it looks. Why didn't you just call us instead of hiding the remains?"

She shrugged. "I dunno. I figured I couldn't beat the rap, so why try. It didn't look good both were dead."

"Any idea why he'd kill his own sister?"

"Yeah. He was fucking crazy."

"True, he was a homicidal maniac. And a sexual predator. You're lucky to still be alive. His sister was just in love with him, from what he know, and went along to please him. She helped him elude capture for a long time. It's strange he turned on her suddenly."

"So I did you a favor," the bartender said dryly.

"Not your job, so no thanks."

"Right. I just make drinks. Damn good ones, too."

"So we've heard. No more booze where you're going."

"Will I get executed for this?"

"There is no capital punishment in this state."

"Shit. So I'll just get Life."

"Probably, if convicted."

"I wouldn't call that living."

"It was your call. Why did you do it? You have no criminal record. Did you know they were themselves killers?"

"No. Lucky coincidence. For you, anyway. Me, I was just bored."

"We'll see that you get a fair trial, so you can plead self defense."

"Not holding my breath, slick. There ain't no justice in this world. You gotta make your own."

Later that night, she hung herself in her cell. She'd seduced then strangled the female guard on suicide watch, one final fling for the road, and took her belt. She left a note written in the her own blood that read, "*Left the building. Gone to Graceland.*" The guard died with a smile on her face. The bartender simply looked ready to go, like a cup of damn good hot coffee that would cool off way too soon unless it was gulped.

FLESHPOT ORGY

Down below or maybe up above on the rotating ball of dirt and shit, all the sentient meat sacks swilled the sensuous stew of soulless sin, spiked with the passionate poison of ephemeral ecstasy, drunk on their own hubris and hedonism.

The horned, horny demon, his gray, greasy skin dotted with oozing warts, including his throbbing, leaky penis, stirred the vast, steaming cauldron of virtual self-aggrandizing flesh soaking in pungent bodily fluids, thinking of the last human he'd spiritually possessed while weird orchestral synthesizer music echoed throughout his dark, dank chamber of horrors, which approximated Salvador Dali's worst nightmare. The old scopitone "Web of Love" featuring Joi Lansing was perpetually projected from his skull onto the walls, but haphazardly, so it was stretched out like a reflection in a funhouse mirror. How he loved these beings of fragile flesh, and the melodious music they made. It was only through their puny but hypersensitive bodies he could fully enjoy the pleasures of physical intimacy.

Recently, he lost his most cherished love object, because inexplicably and without precedent, her powers of domination proved greater than his. This devastated his spirit and diminished his ability to fully disguise himself. Now he had to settle for carnal compensation via many other, lesser vessels.

Of course, the raw, writhing ingredients of his ersatz stew were merely shadowy figments of his fevered, perversely eroticized imagination, floating in a thick, bubbly broth blending blood, urine, sweat, and semen, since human bodies and the Earth itself were primarily composed of liquid elements. This was his constant Unhappy Hour cocktail. He could see the little shadow meat puppets, sense them, but could not touch or devour them. These imaginary bodies were not real, so their non-existent souls were not trapped in torment. Contrary to mythical rumor, the demon did not have any power over the soul. In fact, the demon himself wasn't sure he even possessed a soul, but no matter, since he was already inexplicably immortal.

Every now and then he would dip a bony finger into the broth and lick the concoction, but there was no taste other than sense memories, because he was merely gazing down at a reflection of a reality he could no longer engage with, only witness from a distance. It was a mirror pool of his endless discontent, only made manifest via vicarious vehicles outside of his private sanctuary.

He masturbated into the cauldron, and the ghostly occupants seemed to revel in the additional savory fluid gushing from his weeping cock. Tears of blood streamed down his hideous face and muscular chest and veiny loins and then eventually flowed into the massive cauldron as well. But there was no release for him. For whatever reason, he was doomed to an eternity of voyeuristic torture, at least in between random abductions of those corporeal beings susceptible to his powers of hypnotic hallucination, seduced by promises of perpetual sensual indulgence without price or penance.

It wasn't always like this, though. Once, he had

been an angel, or so the fairy tale goes, who fell in love with a beautiful human woman, which was not part of the fairy tale. It didn't go so well, though. Then as an accursed demon he fell in love again, with another female human, and another and another until he finally ran into Her at a strip club. That didn't turn out to his advantage, either. It just made everything worse, robbing him of his one compensatory talent: to merge and mingle with mankind at will, his true appearance hidden beneath a living lie, all perception of him hidden via hypnosis.

Now he was sentenced to this predatory state of opportunistic body snatching, or rather, corporeal conscience/consciousness-co-opting, essentially erasing the target's sense of moral responsibility to others, making them operate based solely on their most primal instincts, satisfying lustful urges and normalizing abusive behavior, while simultaneously sating the ungodly thirsts of the demonic entity imposing his will on them. Once their souls vacated their own vessels, he likewise lost his control over their destinies. Where they went after the possession, nobody seemed to know, despite the most educated guesses by esteemed philosophers and theologians. Not even the horned, horny demon, who sees all but feels nothing unless he finds and inhabits the weak and unwitting.

Meantime, in between possessions, he masturbated to memories of his many violently sexual trysts in semi-human form over the centuries, up to and including Her. Sometimes he watched his favorite film, Andrzej Zulawski's *Possession* (1983), starring Isabelle Adjani, because it reminded him of the life and love he once had, and would never have again.

Then one day while stirring his pot of salacious fantasies, he came upon a solution: to kidnap as many flesh-pods as possible, bringing them to his lair, giving them eternal life so they'd never die, therefore never escape his clutches. All he had to do was fill them continuously with his sperm, which contained the mysterious elements that sustained his ghastly form, and their's by extension, as it were.

Now, when up among the mortals, he had to stick to the shadows as much as possible, keeping his terrifying form out of sight, then literally grab and drag his selected specimens below to his domain. Sometimes he was seen, but was dismissed as a drug-induced mirage or urban legend. The ones that went missing just stayed that way, forever.

At first he plucked his victims from their daily routines regardless of gender, race, or attractiveness, merely for the sake of experimentation. Most died quickly and horribly under his auspices, or rather their bodies abruptly expired, either during the act of forced fornication with this well-endowed, voracious rapist-demon, or out of sheer fear of his horrific appearance and the ominously oppressive environs, which resembled an expressionistic, cavernous, fire-lit torture chamber, filled with luminous shadows, bizarrely shaped objects dangling from an unseen ceiling, echoing with the screams of souls still trapped within these grisly confines, as yet unable to escape into the vast, endless realm where life and death comprise an inevitable cycle and ironically, emancipation from this claustrophobic Hell.

This was initially frustrating to the demon, but after

much trial and error at the expense of many innocent lives, he collected a group of voluntary vessels willing to live or at least exist eternally in exchange for copious copulation with the demon, and each other. Once these experiments succeeded, he disposed of the ones that did not suit his exact needs. Eventually, all of his remaining sublime subjects were carbon copies of his one true lost love, so that he may have her again and again, with extras to spare. He searched far and wide to find female humans who fit this description, subjecting them to the ultimate and often fatal objectification of the female form. Their ages, skin color and body weight were less important than facial features. They just had to possess the lost love's basic contours and vaguely familiar visage, so that he could dream they were her as he fucked them, his eyes closed in rapture as he filled their barren wombs with his seedless fountain-of-youth semen, since normal, healthy sperm itself was the source of all life on Earth. Furthermore, when he furiously fucked them, one by one or often many at once, the pus oozing from the torn warts on his cock were likewise composed of these beneficial agents. Sharing his essence with these mortal clones of his beloved finally gave him a sense of peace and purpose, which had eluded him for eons.

While in their lovely company, the demon dressed in a dark blue pinstripe suit and two-toned shoes, and adopted a thin mustache, which he applied via illusionary magic, his specialty, though it was now only possible within the confines of his lair, since losing his love meant losing his black magic in the outer realm. The vintage suit was a visage he had seen in an ancient animated film, while inhabiting the body of a prostitute during the Great Depression, who was eventually found guilty of numerous murders and electrocuted by the state. He wanted to make his guests more comfortable around him, showering them with familiar luxuries. He offered them the most glamorous gowns, high-heeled shoes, flimsy lingerie and ostentatious jewelry to wear as they lounged around his own hellish bachelor pad, at least when not naked and soaking inside and out with demonic juices. Of course this was mainly for his own fetishistic pleasure, but as long as he kept their senses sated, the arrangement was mutually pleasing.

He supplied them with an endless assortment of food and drink, mostly premium alcohol served in coup glasses, though while trapped, or rather, semi-willfully confined within these chambers, their beautiful bodies required no sustenance beyond his milky semen or the vile but healthy fungus emanating from his busted penile pustules. They consumed these earthly sub-stances out of sheer gluttony. None of the food or drinks were real, so their consumption had no benefits or consequences other than intoxication. It was all part of the show that must go on without end. The orchestral synthesizer music played non-stop in the background as they fed and fucked, fed and fucked, fed and fucked. It was like a Boris Vallejo painting brought to vivid life.

Eventually the women grew weary of the constant, monotonous background music and the demon went topside and fetched an old-fashioned Victrola and some scratchy 78rpm jazz records, giving his lair the feel of a Prohibition-era brothel. This lasted a while, until it didn't. The impermanence of gratitude and satisfaction amongst his guests was not lost on him, and he grew worried.

The women began making love with each other almost exclusively, as he watched and masturbated. They seemed to enjoy this diversion from the routine, but only grudgingly endured his eventual participation. They'd rather sit and watch his collection of Betty Boop cartoons, beamed from his brain.

The demon feared they were suffering the same affliction as the late Seattle bartender, whom he had briefly possessed on a whim due to her innate promiscuity, which was eventually poisoned due to chronic ennui which turned into fatal malaise. He could never die of boredom, however, since his immortality came equipped with mental and physical stamina impervious to time or repetition. But his guests now obviously saw themselves as prisoners, not guests in his pornographic underground resort. One by one, they begged for release, and when he refused, they escaped the only way they knew how, intentionally choking to death on his cock as the suddenly toxic organic fluids filled their lungs and stomachs, or bursting like globs of goo when he penetrated their orifices with his magnificent member and filled them with his once invigorating liquid beyond human capacity.

Worst of all, he came to realize that many imposters did not add up to the singular ecstasy of embracing his one true lost love. The substitution of promiscuity for purity was unsustainable, as was this so-called solution to his dilemma.

Bottom line: Humans were not built for eternity, either internally or externally. The forces of Nature had defeated his evil intentions. His powers were limited to his own isolated kingdom where he will wallow in his own filth forever. For reasons never sensibly explained to him by anyone or anything, he was condemned to a never-ending life of lonely listlessness. He tossed out the old jazz 78s and replaced them with a LP of "Intermezzo from Cavalleria rusticana" by Italian composer Pietro Mascagni, which played on a continuous loop as he moped in his celibate solitude between fornicating forays topside, penetrating the souls and obliterating the earthly existence of those he possessed as well as their own victims, perpetuating the pointless cycle of pleasure and pain.

All humanity must continue to suffer if his misery had no end, he decided. His lack of empathy for other sentient beings was the source of endless, abject agony. But he didn't care. Because as a spiritual advisor once told him, just before her own brutal murder, only sociopaths value power over others at the expense of their own souls, willfully unaware that their so-called curse is self-inflicted.

LIKE, DIG

The killer flooded the veins and orifices of his victims to overflow with his toxic fluids. But he could never fill the void within, which only deepened after each excursion into malevolent madness.

He didn't commit these atrocities because of a traumatic childhood or sublimated rage or demonic possession, as depicted in the many grindhouse movies he'd seen, back in New York. He did it because he wanted to, because he could, just like the freaks in his two favorite films, *Last House on the Left* (1972) and *I Spit On Your Grave* (1978). That was it. Or at least that's how he justified his venal actions, simply by not offering any defense or excuse, at least to himself. This was how he could continue without conscientious interference.

Perhaps the killer lacked a soul, which accounted for the void within. That's what a priest told him once, but he just punched the priest in the pew and left. He definitely had no heart, other than the piece of meat beating in his chest with fluctuating regularity like a rusty machine. Maybe it had something to do with the fact he suffered from the rare hormonal disorder called acromegaly, like 1940s B movie actor Rondo Hatton, disfiguring his face and parts of his body with hideous lumps. As the disease progressed throughout his puberty, he was shunned by his peers, particularly girls. But there was a sickness in his soul that became evident long before it manifested outwardly.

When he was a kid, sad songs didn't make him cry, only laugh, and he tortured animals. There was no rational explanation for this behavior, which only worsened as he entered young adulthood, and he didn't need or want one. This was just how he was made. He not only accepted it, he embraced it as his true identity. It gave him a sense of purpose and focus.

After the first time he was incarcerated as a teenager for numerous charges including assault and battery, public masturbation, and violent home invasions, he was sentenced to the psych ward at a local hospital, rather than jail, since he was deemed mentally unstable and unfit to stand trial. His real and foster families were all dead or mysteriously missing. He was all alone in the world.

This was where he was treated by a beautiful female psychiatrist with long, flowing brown hair, big blue pools sparkling beneath her cat-eye glasses, and a hidden scientific agenda. Initially she had diagnosed him as a sociopath with violently misogynistic tendencies, but eventually she upgraded him to schizoid misanthrope, since he didn't seem to discriminate between the sexes with his disdain. But he was much worse than either designation, because he was prone to act on his misdirected hatred and primordial lusts. The way he figured it, he was one of Nature's high-level predators. This self-proclaimed status placed him in the hierarchy among the many competitive species inhabiting this dark, angry planet that kept spinning around a blazing ball of hot gases in a cold, merciless black void, the same void which echoed and reflected within him. All living things fought for their lives for no good reason other than to merely exist for its own sake. Because they feared the finality of death, which was inevitable, anyway. His role was to merely expedite the process, so he might as well enjoy it, too. There was no higher power calling the shots, no presiding judge, no final justice. No karma, no kismet, no predetermined destiny. He was free to run amok with impunity, no redemption required. The beautiful psychiatrist found his nihilistic philosophy both alarming and intriguing.

Insanity ran in his family like a wild beast on the loose at a garden party, determined to destroy all remnants of serenity. The beautiful psychiatrist discovered this background via personal research and multiple interviews with the young future killer. He couldn't help it. He was both circumstantially and biologically cursed, simply following his base instincts and natural impulses, or that's what he told her, since he figured that's what she wanted to hear, and pleading insanity had kept him out of prison, at least so far. The psychiatrist tentatively agreed, but still insisted it was all mainly due to genetics, not environmental factors, since many people had fucked up families, but didn't wind up as criminals (unless you considered politicians), just artists, or psychiatrists, like her. In a way, she related to him, even empathized with him. He intentionally misinterpreted her keen interest in his welfare as erotic love, but kept this fantasy to himself, at least at first.

Explaining she had discovered a pioneering way to correct this psychological malfunction, she coerced him into hypnosis, with the aid of a special drug, her very own concoction, which she injected into his blood without telling him what it really was, or at least, what it was meant to be and do. Then, once he was under its insidious influence, she asked him to count backwards from one hundred, and by the time he reached zero, he had completely reverted to his dormant primal state, the same primordial personality that resided within us all, as she was determined to prove to a skeptical medical community that deemed her not only unorthodox, but unhinged. Only her mesmerizing physical allure saved her from losing her license to practice, since even in that lofty field, empowered men with ultimate authority were very shallow when it came to sex.

Her goal was to reset the future killer's very nature by wiping the biologically tainted slate clean and starting from scratch. Since this theory made no sense to her colleagues, she had to implement it clandestinely, under the cloak of a routine session in a part of the hospital only the bravest doctors dared venture. For this, she required a very specific kind of patient, predisposed to sensual aggressiveness, but relatively easy to manipulate. The young future killer fit this bill perfectly, she believed.

But the experiment backfired immediately with a tragic twist of irony. While under the spell of this radical procedure, its premiere trial run on a human subject, the future killer made her his very first victim, sexually assaulting then strangling her in her office, escaping out the window, taking her notebook of secret methodology with him, as well as a sample of the formula. He studied the notebook carefully, absorbing the information easily since he possessed a high degree of intelligence despite his lowbrow lifestyle, and learned how to replicate her experiments on others, duplicating her mind-control alchemy with the same blend of chemicals, easily obtained via illegal channels.

Once the homicidal sex fiend had learned all he needed to know, he began kidnapping and subjecting his chosen victims to the same drug-induced hypnotic regressive therapy techniques the late psychiatrist had employed, forcibly injecting them with the hallucinogenic serum so the woman, selected for their extreme attractiveness, would be not only compliant, but enthusiastic, since they had likewise been lulled into a primeval state of savage sensuality, voraciously anxious to mate with this brutish caveman. He pretended they were organically enamored with him, in order to emotionally compensate for a lifetime of rejection by the opposite sex, attributed to his diseased countenance. He needed no justification for his own depraved cravings, though some things the psychiatrist said to him had rattled whatever semblance of a conscience he might've had, hence this "date rape" alternative, which was not morally superior, certainly, but functionally more humane, or at least that's how he chose to see it. The killer never needed to inject himself with the anthropological aphrodisiac agent again, since he was already perpetually primitive in his attitudes and behavior.

Tragically, his victims never came out of their eroticized trances, unless they woke up somewhere in a fabled afterlife, because he always brutally strangled them when their bestial copulation was completed to mutual satisfaction, in fact in the middle of their final orgasm, so at least they'd die while experiencing the illusion of physical ecstasy. For them, the two constants, sex and death, had tragically merged, and they died not even knowing the difference.

The reason he resorted to killing his victims was because he was afraid if he just left them alive, they might not only identity him in a court of law—and his features were hard to confuse with anyone else's—but he might impregnate them. He did not want to propagate his pain or spawn any more malformed malcontents into this world. This was his single act of relative compassion, if one didn't count the murders.

Before ending their lives and any chance of mutated offspring, the killer always imposed his lifelong foot fetish on his artificially enraptured victims, sucking their toes and licking their feet as he violated their vaginas, ejaculating all over their bodies while they laughed and laughed, oblivious to his ultimate intentions, their civilized inhibitions suppressed by the drug which from their point of view morphed his monstrousness into macho sex appeal. This delusion made the experience relatively enjoyable for them, as well as for the killer, even if was all a vicious lie.

The killer's murderous rape rampage went on for years without a blip or glitch until the rabid dog bite. While ferociously fucking his latest victim, bringing them both to repeated orgasms, a large dog jumped up out of nowhere and attacked him from behind. At least he assumed it was a dog, judging by the growls and gashes inflicted on his neck and back. However, shadows on the wall reflected a much more humanoid shape, but the killer was in too much pain to consider this cognizant conflict carefully. The intruding presence seemed to engulf him, so that the dog-monster seemed like it was all over him and within him, too. In fact, it was as if the thing had broken out of a crate inside his head, then dug a deep crater in his consciousness from which his long-buried conscience occasionally seeped out.

After mauling the killer from without and within, the ferocious dog-monster fled, virtually disappearing from the dark, otherwise empty house. Badly wounded, the killer could not complete his current task, and so he limped out, not only leaking a trail of DNA evidence in his wake, as usual—since all of his victims were left full of unidentifiable drugs and copious amounts of semen—but this time, leaving behind a living witness as well. This would make him easier to find, he presumed, despite his efforts to conceal his identity and location from the police. The killer never used a blade or other weapon that could be traced back to him, only the brute strength of his massive hands, and he moved continuously, all around the gloriously gloomy Pacific Northwest, living in cheap hotel rooms under assumed names and stolen cash and credit cards. His intimidating appearance, threats of violence and bribery assured him many underground accomplices.

Since the one live victim was still groggy and giggling from the mysterious drug (remnants of which were found in the syringe the killer left behind, swabbed for forensic study), all she could describe were her attacker's enormous penis, misshapen torso, hairy chest and back, and long, wet tongue voraciously slobbering all over her face, throat, torso and legs as she undulated with forbidden pleasure beneath his powerful, hirsute bulk. But throughout the ordeal, the brute's face remained a nightmarish blur. What she didn't know was that his face even appeared this way to himself in the mirror, his already grotesque features apparently shifting randomly, creating alternate identities for himself, which came in handy, given his occupation. This was another reason the cops had trouble finding him.

Oddly, in the police report, the victim recalled her rapist screaming out something about being bitten by an animal attacking him, specifically a dog, but she confessed she didn't have a dog, did not see one during the ordeal, and had no idea where an alleged canine savior might've come from, though someone or something had obviously intervened on her behalf, since the rapist had suddenly stopped and ran out, shrieking in agony. She assumed if it had been a dog, it must have belonged to a neighbor, and had escaped its confines. However, no one could theorize how a dog could have entered a locked house, since there were no broken windows, much less its motivation for such bold defense of a total stranger. And no neighborhood dogs exhibited any signs of such a struggle.

Of course, the killer had no knowledge of the report's specific details, other than those describing the bizarre sex acts, since he committed those himself. But he assumed the police now had an eyewitness description and account for the very first time, which would help them match the DNA evidence. The killer's paranoia consumed his consciousness. The authorities were finally on to him directly, thanks to that god damn dog.

It wasn't until the first full moon after the mysterious dog attack that the killer became aware of the changes. He would black out and wake up in the woods, next to a big pile of shit, presumably his own, ensconced in autumn leaves. The first few times he was so disoriented he didn't even know his location, and he had to walk miles until he found a recognizable landmark. His clothes were always tattered, but there were no other signs indicating his condition while under the spell of this mysterious malady.

Assuming he had a brain tumor, another nice gift from the gods, the killer decided to step up the pace of his sexualized slaughter, since apparently he only had so much time left on this miserable plane.

One rainy day several months after the dog bite, while sitting in the Wedgwood Broiler eating his lunch and reading the *Seattle Times*, the killer noticed an interesting item: MYSTERY UNDERDOG TO THE RESCUE. Since no police had yet shown up at his door, the killer had lapsed back into comfortable complacency, while still keeping a low profile, his classic M.O. As usual when he ventured out to public places, the killer wore an overcoat and Fedora hat, the brow pulled down on his forehead, and he always sat in a secluded part of the counter, since his face made him a social pariah. Even the waitress and bartender couldn't make eye contact with him, feigning politeness while repressing their repulsion.

Apparently, according to the newspaper article, a dog walking on two legs was "stalking" the local neighborhoods, but not to terrorize the residents or their pets. He, She, or It was evidently intervening in attempted robberies and rapes and other crimes, viciously dismembering the would-be criminals, allowing the potential victims to flee. Each described what was essentially a canine monster. A werewolf. A werewolf that acted like a superhero. The killer had seen werewolves and superheroes in the movies, and read about them in comic books as a kid. His favorite was *Werewolf by Night*. In fact, the dog-monster resembled that character, at least from what he could tell. Maybe these monsters were truer than he always thought, based on hidden facts that were finally being unearthed for unknown reasons.

There was one other possibility that plagued him, though. Surely, this could not be *me*, the killer thought to himself. It had to be that same rabid beast that attacked him in that girl's apartment. But he couldn't write off the coincidence of the alleged incidents, which all happened to perfectly coincide with his own nocturnal blackouts, while the moon was full.

As the killer pondered the various possibilities, with Sinatra singing on the sound system, he noticed a man sitting right next to him, apparently undeterred by the killer's appearance, humming along to the swingin' tune as he peeked over the killer's hulking shoulder and perused the same newspaper story, casually sipping a three-olive Martini and snacking on a plate of french fries.

"Here, ya want it?" the killer asked the man, hoping he'd take the paper and move down the counter and leave him safely in self-imposed isolation.

"Yeah, sorry for intruding," the man said, not staring directly at the killer's face, but not obviously avoiding it, either. "That story intrigues me."

"Yeah? How come?"

"Well, I walk dogs for a living, for one thing."

"Yeah? What's the other thing?"

"I used to be a private eye, and this is just the sort of case I'd have jumped on back in the day."

"Yeah? Private eye? Didn't know they still made those." Suddenly, the killer was appreciating some non-judgmental company for a change.

"Well, I'm somewhat out of fashion, which is why I quit. One reason, anyway. But then I'm a born anachronism."

"A bored *what*?"

"*Born*. Anachronism. But yeah, I guess 'bored' applies, too."

"I don't know what that means."

"Sometimes I don't know what anything means."

"Amen to that. I don't understand life. Or death. But that's the key: don't try understanding them. Just *do* them. They're both gonna happen, anyway."

"Wow. Kinda heavy topics. Jumping right in."

"Sorry. I guess that article got to me, too."

"Well, at least the innocent people got away."

"Innocent? Who's innocent? We're all guilty of somethin'. Right?"

"I guess. It's all relative."

"Most people who do bad things get away with it. And everybody does bad things."

"That's a cynical viewpoint, pal."

"I'm not your pal. I'm just making an observation. From experience."

"I hear you. To paraphrase Elvis, 'it's just the beast in us.'"

"Elvis? Presley? He said that? When?"

"In the movie 'Jailhouse Rock'."

"Never seen it."

"You should. His best next to 'King Creole.' Though I still dig 'Blue Hawaii' and 'Viva Las Vegas,' too. But start with 'Jailhouse Rock.'"

"Why should I? I lived it."

"You danced in a jail?"

"We're all in jail. Our own personal prisons. Trapped in our own minds. I just break out sometimes."

The man sipped his Martini thoughtfully and ate some more fries. "Well, okay," he said finally, finally feeling visibly uncomfortable.

The killer was worried he was alienating his new friend, and dialed back his animosity. "It's a dog eat dog world, anyway, am I right?"

The man nodded and smirked. "Maybe that's why this wonder dog is out there, bringing justice, old school style. I think dogs are better people than humans, anyway. That's an observation based on *my* own experience."

"Old school?"

"Vigilante."

"But he's a dumb animal."

"Smart enough to get away."

"True. You think maybe he's not an animal? Like a human with fangs?"

"You've seen too many movies, pal. But that's okay. So have I. I dig animals so I naturally dig werewolves. 'I Was a Teenage Werewolf' was my favorite. Also 'The Howling.'"

"Teen Wolf, yeah. You mean the one with Michael Fox?"

The man sighed heavily. "Michael *Landon*."

"Don't know that one, either. Your references are seriously out of date."

"You know, the one where the mad doctor turns the juvenile delinquent into a werewolf with regression therapy."

The killer squinted, sitting up. "With *what*?"

"He hypnotizes the kid so he reverts to his primal state. That's how he becomes a werewolf. It was a unique concept at the time, since before that, most werewolves in movies were the results of supernatural witchcraft, dig? All that gothic jazz. Though to be fair, there was a movie just called 'The Werewolf' that came out the year before, which also made the monster a product of atomic science. Of course, this same basic premise was reused in 'Monster on the Campus,' directed by Jack Arnold, only the regression resulted in a cromagnon, not a lycanthrope, which makes more sense in context, since cavemen were our direct ancestors, not wolves."

The killer squirmed with discomfort, wondering who this guy was, and how he knew so much. Maybe too much for his own good. "You're puttin' me on. How do you know all this shit? It's all such crazy nonsense. Something like that would never work in the real world."

"That's my point. Ain't no such thing as werewolves. Though I get the appeal. I wish I could be a werewolf sometimes. It would get me out of the house and give me something to do at night, anyway. Plus I'd have power over my enemies. I mean, if I had any."

You're making one right now. "Well, maybe your dream will come true someday."

"Yeah? How's that?"

"Why not? Weirder things have happened. Sometimes stuff you see in the movies, they come true." *Case in point*, the killer thought to himself, wondering if that ancient movie had consciously or subconsciously planted a seed in the late psychiatrist's now deceased brain, a seed which had inadvertently sprouted into his current lifestyle.

"Art imitating Life and vice versa, huh?" the man said, interrupting the killer's contemplation of this coincidence which seemed more like an accidental revelation. At least he hoped so, for both of their sakes.

The killer, remembering his fragile state of freedom, decided to play it coy and said, "What do you mean? Art imitating life and vice versa."

"See, when I was a private eye, I had a lot of mundane cases. But the one mystery that always plagued me was this: Is life something that happens to you, or something you make happen?"

"There you go, gettin' all smart with me. I ain't no deep thinker like you. At least, not normally."

"Well, you're right, in movies, people do get away with murder sometimes, and in real life too. Politicians, for instance. Maybe justice really is just a myth. We just like to pretend there's a cosmic balance in the universe."

The killer looked at him with cold suspicion. "What exactly are you gettin' at?"

"Movies are fantasies, man. That's all. Stuff can happen on that side of the screen that can't happen here. Werewolves are one of them, much as I'd like to think otherwise. But other stuff, sex and violence, that's all real. Just not as stylized when they happen in real life. I've seen plenty of both in my line of work, and on the screen. So I know the distinction."

"Line of work. You mean walking dogs?"

"Not walking dogs, like the one in the story. Dog

walking."

"You know what I mean. You into animals, like kinky farmers?"

The man rolled his eyes. "Being a professional peeping Tom is what I meant. I'm retired from that racket now, though. I've seen enough."

"I haven't. I can't get enough."

"Of what, sex and violence?"

"Yeah."

"You mean in movies."

The killer shrugged. "Why settle for the fake stuff when you can have the real thing? See, regular people, they justify bad things in movies, get off on it even, but not in real life. I call that, whaddya call it. Hypocritical."

"Real life has consequences. Movies don't. But I get your drift. That's why we have Art. So we can sublimate our primal instincts creatively, without justifying them in polite society. Nobody gets hurt that way. You don't dig any holes you can't climb out of. It's all make believe."

"You sure talk a lot for a dog walker."

"Well, I think a lot. Lots of time for that, doing what I do."

"I guess my real point is, there's so much sex and violence in this world already, way more than in movies. I prefer the real world for that reason. It's our nature, to be this way. It's even in an animal's nature. We fuck and we kill. It's how the real-world works. Movies just try to make it pretty. It ain't."

"I hear you. I watch a lot of violent movies, too. I love sex and violence when it's fantasy. I love sex when it's real, too. Not a big fan of violence in real life.

Funny how in this culture, paying to watch people kill each other in a movie is acceptable, but watching two people make love in a movie is considered taboo. Im other words, inflicting pain is good, sharing pleasure is bad. Totally screwed up and backwards, in my opinion."

"So you don't like violence, unless it's fake."

"Yeah, I dig a good gunfight or slasher like anybody else. I'd rather look at tits, though, frankly. All due respect for women. I wish one would be president already."

"Yeah, I love sex. And violence. I especially like it when they're combined. *That's* what *I* call our primal nature."

"Well, like I said, that's what movies are for. A safe outlet for those primitive instincts and impulses."

"So you're a hypocrite like everyone else. But trust me. You and me, we're more alike than you want to admit. I just fulfill my natural needs. You suppress them."

"No, I just indulge in casual sex, so nobody gets hurt. My heart gets busted a lot anyway, but I'm used to that, and it's my own fault, I've learned the hard way, for getting too attached too quickly, to just about anyone that'll have me. But that's no excuse for causing someone else pain. It's called empathy. It's a quality many people lack. I'm glad I don't."

"Fuck empathy. It's a dog eat dog world, like I said. *You* should know that."

"True enough. But still, I mind my own business, and messing with other people's peace and privacy and right to exist on their own terms only gives me problems I don't need. I dig that people fundamentally suck. But most people are innocent of being a monster, at least."

"Look, *everyone* is guilty, and they deserve what they get."

The man really noticed the man's ugliness for the first time and nodded blankly. Then he gulped down the rest of his Martini, looked at his phone and said, "Well, I gotta split. Dogs to walk, all that jazz. You have a nice day, pal."

"Fuck you too," the killer muttered while nodding with fake politeness, Seattle-style. "Hypocrite."

Something strange if not sinister had infiltrated the killer's soul via this man's presence and proximity, an unfamiliar interloper he did not recognize. It scared him, and he never got scared, because he was the bringer of fear, not the recipient, for that was his natural born role in this world, to dominate and destroy. It wasn't supposed to bother him, because he was only being true to himself.

The next day the ex-private eye returned to the Wedgwood Broiler for his regular meal, Martinis and french fries, since he was a vegan now. Along with his own newspaper, he had brought an old book of Elmer Batter photographs, so he could peruse vintage photos of feminine feet and legs adorned in nylons and high heels. Normally he reserved these erotic images for private time alone at home, a harmless release for his fetishistic desires, but lately his loneliness was bothering him more than usual, probably why he had struck up a conversation with a total stranger, something he normally did not do. He almost hoped that weird guy from yesterday was there again, since on some base level, he felt a kinship with him, and wanted to find out what it was. And for some reason, he had trouble remembering what he looked like, other than he was obviously suffering from some sort of genetic defect, which only engendered sympathy, not revulsion. It reminded him of Jack Arnold's 1955 sci-fi horror classic *Tarantula*, wherein the mad scientist was forcibly injected with his own formula that inadvertently caused a form of acromegaly in humans, and gigantism in animals, particularly the titular creature. The stranger also sadly resembled the actor Rondo Hatton, tragic star of *House of Horrors* and *The Brute Man* (both released posthumously in 1946). In fact, the ex-private eye felt bad for referencing the caveman in *Monster on the Campus*, since the stranger himself looked like a mutated throwback. That was probably why he'd decided to offer him company, and perhaps a semblance of solace. The ex-private eye always felt an affinity for outcasts, though normally the four-legged variety. They were lower maintenance. His favorite movie line of all time was from his favorite B movie, *I Was a Teenage Werewolf* (1957): "People bug me."

The strange stranger wasn't there, though, which was both a disappointment and a relief. He was better off by himself. He loved the Wedgwood Broiler because it felt perpetually stuck in the previous mid-century. Most of the bars he frequented had that timeless ambience. It was his way of beating time, and sometimes making time. Whatever he had in common with the stranger wasn't enough to form a bond, that was for sure. Besides, he had his eye on the red-haired waitress's lovely gams, and was preparing to finally ask her out. She reminded him of actress Tina Louise, though there was some projected embellishment involved. It was just as well he could proceed with his designs on her sans any interference, since it wasn't just the old music and wood-paneled coziness that appealed to him. She was one of the reasons he kept coming back, too. He was obsessed with her face and her feet, but then he was a serial obsessor. Life wasn't worth living unless he was infatuated with a woman. This relentless desire for female companionship at all costs had been his curse since he was a kid. And that's exactly how he saw it, a curse. A shrink once told him he was a sex addict, in addition to being an alcoholic. As a result, the man even attended SLAA meetings. But all he wound doing was cruising the other attendees. He knew there was something wrong with him, besides his foot fetish, which Quentin Tarantino shared, after all. He even saw Will the Thrill and Monica Tiki Goddess playing footsies on HBO's *Reel Sex* years ago. Anyway, he had an insane mother and abusive father and a brother who committed suicide, so he could be much worse. Whatever his innate neuroses, he had learned to accepted them, more or less without question. The way he saw it, no one was getting hurt, but him.

So the man settled in on a cloudy afternoon with the sounds of Sinatra, his Martini, and basket of french fries for company, wondering if he should give the waitress the poem in his pocket, or just ask her out directly.

However, the man soon discovered that the stranger would indeed be intruding on his consciousness, but this time from a safe if disturbing distance. It was all right there in the paper, which the man picked up after he couldn't take any more photos of 1960s women's lovely arches. There he saw the stranger's horrifying face, essentially a posthumous mug shot, next to an article about how he was a suspect in multiple rapes and murders, but someone had done the cops' job for them. The M.O. was oddly familiar, too.

The killer had apparently torn out his own throat after digging his own grave and lying in it. Oddly, the ex-private eye was not shocked, only saddened. The killer's better nature, his inner animal, ultimately eliminated the aching void by destroying the possessive demon lurking within. The ex-private eye had seen it before. It happened all the time.

Another case solved, if only by proxy, without even trying, like one of his heroes, *Kolchak: The Night Stalker*. Now on to the next impossible challenge. The ex-private eye reached in his pocket and pulled out the poem.

THE FLEETING FEELING OF FOREVER

The lovers felt entwined for eternity until the thread was pulled and it all began to unravel like an insecurity blanket woven from willful self-delusion.

Still in a post-coital state of bliss, the woman sat up, picked up and popped open her laptop from the beside table, and began idly perusing the local news headlines. She felt both uncomfortable and unsatisfied after sex with her current partner, so this was a way of distracting herself, while heading off any obligatory chit-chat or worse, cuddling. She'd rather ponder her prospects for a better future, preferably alone, or at least unshackled by dead emotional weight.

This train of thought was abruptly sidetracked.

Horrified, she read aloud the story of the "werewolf rapist," who had just been found dead from an apparent grisly suicide. Her groggy but aroused boyfriend seemed quite intrigued as she conveyed some of the more lurid details of the assaults, related to authorities by the lone survivor who had been rescued by a mystery dog hero, the one apparently responsible for numerous recent interventions on behalf of crime victims. As she told her boyfriend all the horrible things that had been done to this poor woman, particularly the foot licking, he began to masturbate, and suddenly wanted to make love again. The woman was disgusted. She saw her boyfriend clearly for the first time: he was no different from the werewolf rapist. He was simply too cowardly to act out his own prurient fantasies. So she reached into her beside drawer, pulled out a pair of sharp scissors normally used for knitting and cat claw trimming, and in one savage motion cut off her boyfriend's recently drained but re-erected cock. While he crouched in agony screaming and bleeding, she flushed the evidence down the toilet (having learned a thing or two from historical precedent) on her way out the door, instinctively heading to the one place where she'd be given a temporary safe haven, her lesbian girlfriend's apartment, where she always kept some stuff, just in case of such an eventuality. Which was always on the agenda, or had been for a while, anyway. Leaving the hunky creep, not emasculating him, but it yielded the same basic result, if with unplanned complications. The werewolf rapist had inadvertently expedited the inevitable next move in her own situation. Hearing about the rapes had exposed the demons residing within her abruptly ex-boyfriend, and for that, at least, she was grateful. It brought to a boil a long simmering decision to change her entire life, rather than just ending it.

Her lesbian lover, a stunningly sensuous, effortlessly elegant African American who sang jazz tunes in nightclubs professionally, lived in Portland. She was like an impossible combination of Pam Grier and Sarah Vaughan. After texting her a heads up, the woman boarded a train and met her at Union Station. They had a celebratory reunion/emancipation date at their favorite spot, cocktails in the Driftwood Room followed by dinner at Gracie's in the Hotel Deluxe, where they often trysted, but not this time. After they ate and drank they went home to the lover's apartment, and made love there. This was where the fugitive woman would be staying, indefinitely. Maybe forever, however long eternity lasted in quantified temporal terms, anyway.

"Do you feel bad about what you did?" the lover asked the woman as she unhooked her bra and began nuzzling her erect nipples.

"No. He was thinking about getting a vasectomy anyway," the woman replied casually as she reached her fingers into her lover's wet pussy, eliciting a gasp.

"So he jerked off to you describing the rape?" the lover said later, after they both climaxed and were chatting in bed, something the woman actually enjoyed with this particular person. "That's so *sick*."

The woman lit a cigarette, took a drag and said, "Well, he used to jerk off to me telling him about us fucking, too. He was a sick bastard. Such a nice body, though. Plus he was paying the bills since I lost my fucking stupid job a few months ago. Not worth the plentiful pussy and copious cock-sucking he got in exchange. I'm nobody's whore. Unless I say so."

The lover, ignoring the pang of jealousy, drenched in carnal sweat, sat up and said, "What? You told him about us? He knew?"

"Yup."

"And he didn't care?"

"Nope."

"Wow. Well, I'm glad we're both rid of him now. We can be together at least, without worrying. Forever."

The woman nodded but didn't say anything. The knot in her stomach when her lover said the word "forever" made her quiet and pensive.

Later that night, they lay in bed watching the 1982

film *The Beastmaster,*

"My ex used to play this as we made love," the woman said. "Over and over and over. Because he thought I looked just like Tanya Roberts in this movie."

"You do," her lover said as she went down on her, bringing her to orgasm before the favor was returned.

"I just like the animals," the woman said as they lay together, just as she had done with the man she had left behind in a pool of his own blood. It felt like nothing had changed, or would ever change. This is how it would be forever: a constant, relentless drip-drip-drip of delirious decadence until it all got sucked down the drain of disillusionment and finally death, the only permanent relief. Meantime, it was just a series of moments—both mundane and monumental, but mostly mundane—dissipating instantly into memory, like ice cubes tossed into a sizzling skillet. Maybe this thing with her female lover would work out as a long term, mutually beneficial and harmonious relationship. Maybe it wouldn't. Odds were roughly even at best. She only knew one thing for sure: Later always gets here sooner than you think. Best to hedge one's bets because there was no such thing as "inevitable," except when it came to death. Meantime, all we have are these millions of melting, melding moments, ultimately resulting in a moribund mosaic of our own mortality.

At least Death was reliable. Not much else in Life could make that claim.

"I feel like I just woke up from one fever dream into another," the woman said to her lover the next morning, but her lover was still asleep, lost inside her own subconsciousness, unaware of the alternate corporeal reality surrounding her, unhurriedly awaiting her return.

The woman got up to make her breakfast. Unlike any of her recent lovers, she was a vegan, so she often had to cook her own meals separately, and when they went on dates, she was the fussy one about the menu, always demanding "cruelty-free," customized options. Right now she just threw together into a sizzling skillet some chopped mushrooms, onions, garlic, tomatoes, and tofu her lover kept stocked in the fridge for the rare times she could get away. Now that she was free, the fridge would require more of these plant-based dietary choices. If her lover didn't like it, she would leave her, the woman thought. She really felt no attachment to any human being. She missed her cat, who had been lost for the past week. Her ex said he looked around but could never find the cat. The woman put up flyers around the neighborhood, but no response. Now that she'd fled her own crime scene in Seattle, she'd probably never see her cat again. She'd already changed her cell phone number. Her ex probably called the cops from the hospital (she'd done him the courtesy of anonymously dialing 911, at least). He knew she had a lesbian lover, of course, but he didn't know where she lived. At least, the woman never told him. He'd have to hire a private dick, especially now that he was missing his own. She wasn't worried about it. She wasn't worried about anything, except her cat. Everything else would be settled in due time. Nothing lasts forever. It only feels that way sometimes.

That night they were having cocktails at another of their favorite hangouts, The Alibi, an old school tiki bar/restaurant and local institution, cavernous yet cozy, when the woman read about herself in the paper. She saw a photo of her ex, at least his face, along with a picture of hers. This was why she was wearing a red wig in public. The Alibi was also dark, so they felt safe for now. And the lover was picking up the tab, too. For now.

"We should move to another state," the woman's lover said as she sipped her sweet tropical drink from a glass garnished with a tiny umbrella. "I can gig anywhere. I will take care of you."

"I can take care of myself, thank you. And I like the state I'm in."

"Panic?"

"Do I look panicked to you?"

"No, but I am. I don't want to lose you."

"Everybody loses everybody eventually. No one lasts forever, as Oingo Boingo once pointed out."

"It feels like forever sometimes."

"Only for a little while."

"Don't you feel bad at least?"

"About what?"

"Chopping his cock off like it was a slab of beef!"

"He wishes. More like a turkey head. Okay, maybe a modest cucumber. Sorry, I'm vegan, remember, which impacts my foodie references. Nice pecs, though. Anyway, you asked me this already. I'm not going to suddenly get stricken by a crisis of conscience, so forget it. No redemption, but no regrets, either. He got exactly what was coming from him. Probably just another frustrated rapist. I saved a lot of women a lot of trouble."

"So that's why you did it?"

"In retrospect, I suppose. Honestly, I was acting on

instinct and impulse. But it made sense in the moment and it makes even more sense now. The man had no basic empathy. I can't stand people with no empathy. So he paid for his perverse fascination with people's pain the hard way. It was hard at the time, anyway. Made for a nice, clean slice."

"But who is paying the price?"

"He did, with his precious dick. I still got all my junk."

"But not peace of mind."

"Oh, yes I do. More than ever."

"I find that hard to believe."

"Then don't."

"What even made you think of it? I mean, how is that a rational response, no matter how fucked up his reaction to that rape? Men are pigs. We both already know this."

"Shut up. That's not fair. I like pigs."

"But not ham, pork or bacon."

"You do, though."

"I'm sorry."

"I forgive you."

"Promise?"

"For now."

"Then please answer my question."

"Which is what, again?"

"*Why this?*" The lover picked the orange straw out of her drink and bit it in two for visual aid. She had powerful jaws which she often put to good use, and not just vocally.

The woman let out an annoyed sigh and said, "Remember that story about the bride who went on a rampage, fucking all these guys who then let her cut their cocks off without complaint, basically volunteering them in exchange for one quick shot of pleasure inside her beautiful body?"

"Um, no."

"Hm. I could've sworn I read that somewhere. Or saw it in a movie, maybe. Must be an urban legend. It all seemed so real at the time I heard it, in any case."

"Maybe you dreamed it."

"Maybe. Anyway, apocryphal or not, I found the story inspirational. In fact, it also inspired this other woman to kill both her male and female lovers one night, for no apparent reason than she was bored."

"That I read about. Why are you telling me this? Should I be worried?"

"Oh no. I'm not bored. Not yet, anyway. Even if I were, I would never hurt you. You did nothing to deserve it. Though you are a carnivore, but I accept that because most people are meat eaters, since they don't see animals as equals. You'll evolve eventually, but naturally. But that asshole, he definitely did deserve it, and it had nothing to do with how much he fucking loved fucking hamburgers."

"What? How?"

"By being a pervert."

"But sweetie, I'm a little kinky myself."

"Yes, in a normal way. At least around here."

"That sounds boring."

"Not yet."

The lover sipped her drink quietly, contemplating the limitations of their situation with sadness. "I think you need a new identity at least. I know people who can help with that. Then maybe we can go to Canada. I know some people in Vancouver. At least until this dick thing blows over."

"So to speak."

"So you agree?"

"I would like to escape into another body sometimes."

"You can escape into mine anytime."

"Okay, fuck it. Fuck everything and everyone. Let's go home and fuck."

They went home and made hot, sweaty love and fell asleep in each other's arms, as if they would embrace for eternity. But the woman was beginning to feel something worse than ennui. Malaise was settling in and infecting her spirit and warping her perspective. She had to escape before it was too late.

When the woman woke up, a short time later, everything seemed bigger, and strange. Out of proportion. Then she noticed she had four legs and four feet. Actually paws. She was viewing the world through cat's eyes. She hopped up on the bathroom sink and looked in the mirror. She was looking at the face of her own cat. It made her so happy, she licked her own reflection.

Even if she was dreaming with self-awareness, the cat-woman wanted to take advantage of this feline freedom while she could. She slipped out the crack in the kitchen window and ran wild in the streets of Portland. She felt hungry, but since her spirit refused to eat meat, despite her new body's desires and needs, she munched on flowers and shrubs and such. It wasn't long before her spirit merged completely with the cat's consciousness, and they were one and the same, sharing the same consciousness. It was liberating, at least for a while. She felt like she was finally living inside her favorite movie, *Cat People* (1982). The theme song sung by David Bowie was her anthem.

Eventually her cat body died of malnutrition, since it was meant to be carnivorous. She always lamented the fact that cats and dogs had such short lives, which she considered to be one of the true tragedies of life in this world. Now she knew from her brief experience of spiritual cohabitation that they were blissfully unaware of their own mortality, content in the fluid illusion of the passing moments. That's when she woke up from the cat dream, back into her human form. Hardly any time in human terms had passed. She'd been living on cat time.

There were two male cops at the foot of the bed with their guns drawn. Her lover was standing next to them, nude and sobbing, which was distracting the cops. The cat-woman just shrugged, grabbed the scissors out of the drawer in the nightstand, the same pair she'd used to cut her boyfriends' pecker off so the blades were still stained with his blood, and stabbed herself in the throat. She died naked and gurgling gore in her screaming lover's arms, the lover's upturned brown breasts quivering with each sob as the dying cat-woman's wound sprayed and dripped blood all over them. The cops were still momentarily paralyzed with a mixture of lust, shock and horror.

Then the cat-woman passed out and when she opened her gorgeous emerald eyes, or the portals of vision where her emerald eyes had once been, she was wandering, then dancing, feeling emancipated, around the streets of Portland, which now seemed abandoned yet comforting, like an Edward Hopper painting. She felt no hunger, no pain, no desire, no earthly angst. No threats from evil. She didn't even have a body now, human or animal. She only felt the soothing sensation of pure existence for its own sake, without beginning or end since now Time itself had finally lost the illusion of impermanence.

CLAW MARKS ON THE HOURGLASS

Her curvaceous body was being systematically ravaged by the rapist-killer called Time. It was time to emasculate the fucker. The problem was she was suffering from the irreversible human condition of mortality. It was a progressive disease for which there was no cure. The fact it was a universally shared affliction offered no solace or perspective.

For her, success came late to the party. Celebratory appreciation of commercial compensation and material benefits is for the young. Once you're too old to even play the game, the rewards feel more like consolation prizes. She had no use for those, either.

Now she was just another nobody. She hated being a nobody. It was her worst fear next to death, which was inevitable. Both nightmares were coming true, and there was nothing she could do about it.

She didn't fear death. If nothing else, it provided inevitable and permanent emancipation from all neuroses, grief and strife. Mostly she was disturbed by the cruel fragility of Life itself. It just wasn't fair. And she was determined to stop this vicious cycle in its tracks, by any means necessary, even if it all it meant was preserving her own posterity. This had become her mission.

Once, when she was a young Irish Catholic girl, a priest told her to listen to Life. "Maybe the world is trying to tell you something. Or God Himself."

She wasn't having it. "The world isn't trying to tell anyone anything and neither is God Herself. The Universe doesn't give a fuck about us." She quit going to Sunday School shortly thereafter, over the objections of her parents, a standoff which rapidly escalated and resulted with her leaving home altogether and making her own life, her own way, as a willful, sexually liberated teenager. Later, as a prematurely world weary but still youthful woman, she sought solace in psychological treatment, since spiritual sustenance had eluded her. But all shrinks did was repeat back what she had just told them. To her, that racket was nothing but a mind-fuck circle-jerk con job. Just like the religion and entertainment industries, but at least the latter paid her well for her participation.

Another time, one of her many adoring suitors—who only told her exactly what she wanted to hear—strongly suggested that the only solution to depression and anxiety in this world was sex, noting their own congenial genitalia.

"Maybe it's just me," he said.

"Not just you. Just not me." She fucked him anyway, just so he'd go away. When he left, she even felt a little better. At least for a day. Then the darkness fell again. So she kept drinking and fucking, trying to forget her own fate. Nothing seemed to make her feel secure and happy, except her art, and sex was only part of her personal creative expression. She really did think of sex as a natural form of art, and always had, even as a Catholic school girl. That's why and how she became so good at it. It came as easily to her as her johns did under her expert auspices. Sex and art both helped her forget the hard truths of life, even as they both reveled in and revealed it.

Distraction from death was the driving force behind most of human society, or at least that was the conclusion she eventually drew from her strategic vantage point, having met and fucked many, many people of all sexes, colors, tastes, and backgrounds. These distractions came in infinite varieties. Wealth. Entertainment. Competition. Social media. But she had long since realized it was all bullshit. That was the problem. The illusionary veil of life had lifted to reveal a worm-infested corpse lurking beneath, waiting patiently.

She kept a journal, where she wrote random observations, like this one: "The older you get, the more dead people you know and miss and admire, or don't. And with that comes the daily increasing awareness that soon you'll be one of them."

Though nobody read her journal—which she intentionally kept private for now because it was a work in progress, like her life, the ultimate art project—she was hoping it might be discovered someday, probably after her death, which felt both imminent and distant, causing her moods to fluctuate along with her plans for a future that was dwindling daily. She wouldn't know when it would be almost or completely gone until it was too late.

In her will, she left what money she had left in savings from her careers as an exotic dancer and adult film actress to her estranged daughter, along with the journal, in hopes it would be preserved for posterity. This was the real reason she had flown to Seattle to patch things up with her, in order to re-establish some sort of bond. It had gone well, better than expected, despite the fact she impulsively fucked the ex-private eye her daughter had been dating, but it had been a while since her daughter had responded to any emails, text messages, or phone calls. Hopefully her daughter didn't hold that fling against her. She admitted it was an act of competition, and eventually the daughter dismissed it, since she wasn't really in love with the ex-private eye, anyway. Now the mother was worried about her daughter, but much more worried about the custody of her legacy.

She just kept writing, each word composed neatly so it was legible in order to be easily transcribed by whatever publisher won the inevitable bidding war. "Memoirs of a Model Citizen" was one working title. She'd once posed for *Playboy*, during her prime years as a piece of commercial meat. It remained her biggest claim to mainstream fame, other than the underground grindhouse films she'd starred in under an infamous alias, often going so far as to disguise her face with elaborate makeup so her daughter and ex-husband could never find out her dirty but lucrative secret. That line of work had dead-ended years ago, though. Her body was still voluptuous, making her the envy of women years younger, but folds of fat encircled her once flat belly, her large breasts drooped, and her buttocks were far less firm than they'd once been. All she had left to offer of lasting value were her memories, dutifully recorded in her journal without any actual prospects of one day being discovered posthumously. No one was interested in her life while she was still alive, that was for sure.

Most of her films had been released on VHS and a few on DVD, but other than bootlegs, they were all out of print, and naturally they weren't the sort of fare that would be seen on television, even cable or streaming services. Essentially she was already long forgotten, a rotting relic from a bygone era that was receding rapidly into the recesses of pop cultural history, fossils of a dead century and millennium.

But that would change. Everything changes. Without any consent or warning. She forced herself to have faith in a future that would exist without her actual presence, except in literary form. She had no way of predicting this outcome accurately. If no one was interested in her life while she was living it, why should anyone care once she was gone? People are primarily preoccupied with the present, especially when it comes to pop culture. Her contributions were ignored and marginalized from the beginning. The dozens of her pornographic films—many of which she ghost-wrote and directed, shot on 16mm, distributed around New York City, Chicago, Detroit, San Francisco, Los Angeles, Miami, Atlanta, New Orleans, and a few others porn-friendly urban hubs (except Seattle) by the Mob, who also funded them, partly in exchange for sexual favors—had no lingering impact, no rabidly loyal fan base keeping them on life support. They were ghosts themselves. And soon she'd be one, too. Of course, she didn't believe in consciousness outside the corporeal form, so even then, she'd be unable to verify her posterity from beyond the grave. So she chose to simply believe in it now, and enjoy her self-promised posthumous fame while still alive to appreciate it. Even if it wasn't real. Because ultimately, all reality is ephemeral, anyway. At least in the waking world. Perhaps dreams are the true portals to eternity, the true, lasting reality. And in dreams, anything can happen.

For now, she existed in New Orleans, where she had

come to resume her once thriving career as a stripper in New York, after the Mob suddenly stopped funding her films. Her body was still fit and healthy when she'd resumed her stripping career after a long hiatus at age 40, and her nightclub gigs lasted nearly another twenty years. Her reputation around the Big Easy was loud enough that her daughter was able to track her down, via the national stripper network.

Now she was too old even to dance, though she still sold sex to both older and younger men. Primarily fellatio. She was still very skilled at it, and her tongue remained warm and moist, even if her pussy wasn't. She always swallowed too, unless the customer wanted to cum on her breasts, which were still bountiful and beautiful, if soft and saggy. It was a meager income, and she spent most of her earnings on makeup, to cover her face with enough paint that a man would want to put his penis in it, though she also ate pussy for cash, or free booze in one of the several bars she frequented. She was still very good at that, too.

She lived cheaply in a rundown residential hotel on the outskirts of the French Quarter. The owner was an old friend of hers. In fact, he had been in love with her for decades, like countless other men and women. For ten years she didn't pay money for rent, just took it out in trade. But he was old too, and most of the time, he just wanted to cuddle in front of the TV with her. She had free Netflix, too. But he wanted to watch her old films on video with her, over and over, as she went down on him. He was her biggest fan.

One day she was slowly jerking him off to arouse an erection while they watched one of her earliest and most relatively successful films (at least on 42nd Street in Times Square), *Wet Dreams of a Mermaid*, which was also a possible title for her memoirs. For the first time, he came before she had a chance to blow him, then suddenly died from one quick stroke. The lethal kind, that is. She found out the next day he had willed the property to her. She planned to sell it to a developer who wanted to erect condos or a shopping mall, and then move back to Seattle, to be near her daughter, so she could entrust her journals with her in person.

One morning, she was sitting in her favorite spot that wasn't a bar, Cafe du Monde on Decatur Street, breathing in the aromatic humid air, drinking *café au lait* with beignets, writing in her journal, when a young man suddenly sat next to her. She was often recognized by local fans here, and relished the worshipful stares and even the crude gestures, since any attention was better than none.

Or so she thought until the man suddenly spit on her, called her a "whore," and walked away.

She sat there alone, quietly weeping, wiping her cheeks with napkins. A Mexican busboy noticed and offered her more coffee, but she politely declined. He didn't speak much English, but he sensed the source of her suffering. It was the universal language of loneliness.

Afterward she went down to her favorite bar on Bourbon Street and had a Hurricane for lunch. Though it was her favorite bar, she didn't know the name, only the location. Like her, it merely existed, without specific designation, serving its purpose until it was no longer needed. She was surrounded primarily by tourists.

Everyone ignored her. She wasn't even recognized

by the bartender or local patrons. She was like a ghost haunting her own neighborhood.

But she knew she was still alive when two very dirty men sat down on either side of her.

"How much?" one asked.

"For what?" she asked without returning the greasy glare from their hallowed-out faces.

"We know what you are," the other man said. "You're old, used, damaged goods, but you're cheap. Like a thrift shop. We ain't got much to spend, so we'll tell *you* how much. We'll buy you a drink for a blowjob. Both of us."

"But only one drink for both," said the other.

"Yeah, we don't want you to drown."

She nodded as a tear escaped one eye. They bought her another Hurricane, which she sipped slowly. The alcohol always felt like a cleansing rinse.

Then she led them out the back door, and knelt before them. But it didn't go as planned.

The two men beat her, and she scratched at their faces, but they scratched and bruised her worse. They tore off her clothes, forced her to perform oral sex, and were about to rape then kill her in a haze of drunken lust and misdirected rage when a horde of wild cats suddenly engulfed the alley, swarming her attackers, clawing their faces, blinding them as they screamed and finally staggered off in blind agony, eyeballs dangling on their shredded cheeks.

Then they were gone, and she was left alone, again, but this time, it was a relief. Her face and body drenched and caked in tearful mascara, the men's semen and her own blood, she gathered up her torn clothes and staggered home, wondering what had just happened.

There was no scientific, rational explanation for why a pack of stray felines decided to defend her life against violent aggression. There could be theories, some of which may make sense. But things you think are true are only true for a little while, until more facts are revealed. After a long life, though, she had no rationale for her birth or her impending death, much less a heroic intervention by feral cats. There was no sensible reason for anything in this dark dream-world.

Nobody knows what the hell is going on. Nobody. Except maybe the cats. She missed them that night as she cried herself to sleep, and never woke up, her well-worn meat sack finally exhausted beyond further endurance, depleted of all life energy, with her journal, the only lasting proof and potential validation of her relatively brief existence on this plane, lying prematurely unfinished on her bedside table. She slipped quietly into a realm that passed no judgement. For once, even if she was alone, she didn't feel alone. The cats were there, waiting for her.

WET DREAMS OF A MERMAID

In old Times Square, there was no time for squares...

Voiceover: "This is the semi-true fantasy about a woman from the sea who loved seamen, but who could only see men without being seen."

Reel One

She's sprawled out on a turquoise chaise lounge in the home tiki bar that encompasses her entire Manhattan penthouse apartment. The wood-paneled walls are adorned with Polynesian masks, also some African masks since it's all the same to these Caucasian motherfuckers, while tiki statues of all sizes line the hardwood floors. Multi-colored fishing float lights dangle from the ceiling. The bar itself resembles an embedded thatch hut, with bamboo trim and stools. Exotica music by The Out-Islanders is playing from her hi-fi stereo system. Other than her shimmering emerald tail fins, which flip with tantalizing anticipation, she is the epitome of homosapien femininity. Her human half looks rather Asian, perhaps Hawaiian, her long, thick, flowing black hair delicately falling over her alabaster skin, teasingly covering part of her perfectly round, pert, cherry-topped vanilla breasts. The dumpy, drunken man wearing an elaborate fez hat is literally drooling as he removes his silk smoking jacket, slacks, loud aloha shirt, wife-beater undershirt, boxer shorts and socks. Her exotic sensuality is so alluring he involuntarily shoots a geyser of semen all over her fins. She laughs, then gently wipes the substance from her scales and licks it from her fingers. Immediately the man is erect again, but where to put it?

Arms outstretched, the mermaid beckons the man to join her on the luxurious lounge. She lays back so he can mount her. As he devours her soft, organically perfumed flesh, an aperture opens where her crotch would be if she were human, and she gently guides the man's throbbing penis into her piscatorial pussy. He immediately comes again, then passes out cold.

Her tall, muscular, Haitian manservant brings her a Mai Tai in a tiki mug. Only he can offer her true sexual or emotional satisfaction. Rolling the pasty middle-aged white man off of her, she touches the Haitian's hand, signaling to him that she is ready to indulge her own sensual yearnings.

The Haitian is dressed like a jungle warrior, replete with face paint and nose ring, his massive member barely concealed beneath his flimsy loin cloth. She reaches beneath the flap and massages his enormous balls. Instantly his erection pokes from out behind the cloth, and she strokes it with adoration and admiration. The manservant smiles, because now, he is the master. He only pretends to be her manservant for the sake of her paying company, when really, he is her true lover, and they are equals.

He picks her up and she straddles his magnificent figure as he simultaneously slides his monstrous cock into her gaping, dripping aperture, which is already leaking seawater. She screams in her siren language, sounding more like a banshee, as he thrusts harder and deeper. She claws at his broad shoulders as he buries his face in her neck and breasts. Their mouths meet and their tongues explore each other's faces as he cums copiously within her, triggering her own violent spasms of orgasmic release.

Then he lays her back down on the lounge, and he hands her the tiki mug so she may finish her Mai Tai.

"*Next!*" she says, and the door to the apartment opens. Her hired beatnik doorman lets in a slickly attired middle-aged gangster from downtown as the Haitian carries out the previous, still semi-conscious john. The beatnik is wearing the man's fez on the way out, then he puts it back on the john as the Haitian sets him down and props him up against the aqua-blue hallway wall. Meantime, back inside, the sweaty gangster removes his silky suit and jewelry while the manservant makes him a Zombie, his customary cocktail.

The gangster is rough and enthusiastic, but cautious, since all activities here are closely monitored by the manservant, who often joins in when the mermaid entertains female clients. Otherwise he just casually masturbates, ready to intervene if necessary. Anyone who causes trouble meets the end of a spear, or so goes the threat.

The gangster prefers fellatio to intercourse, finding the whole idea of putting his penis in a fish-hole unappealing and creepy. The mermaid is an expert in this carnal art, as the manservant knows too well. She can swallow any man whole. The semen helps sustain her when out of water.

When she's not working, she luxuriates in the large, shadowy indoor saltwater pool adjacent to her apartment, which is dimly lit and lined with bamboo and tikis, where she spends many late nights swimming and frolicking with her manservant, who, like her, is immortal, though he is the product of Voodoo, not Nature. But he is not cursed. He is blessed. He brings her tiki drinks from the poolside bar, as well as seaweed and other vegan snacks from her homeland.

This is her personal paradise on Earth, which is why she is not prepared for the horror that soon will invade her sanctuary from the outside world…

Reel Two

The mermaid's stipulated agreement with her johns (and janes) prohibits them from divulging her whereabouts, much less her existence, to the outside world. She isn't among human civilization to attract public attention. She is here only to make love, love, *love*.

Back in her aquatic kingdom deep, deep below the Bermuda Triangle, the mermaid was courted by many mermen, as well as fellow mermaids, but she craved the human body, and therefore could not be sated by members (as it were) of her own species. Humans were exotic to her. She found them fascinating. Pathetic, yet fascinating.

Of course, the mermaid doesn't trust humans, so the Haitian cast spells on them. They can re-call her address, but could not remember why they go there until they arrive. At a predetermined time each week, they each hypnotically return to her, right on schedule. After each lovemaking session, the selective amnesia returns. But if for some reason one tries to do something sneaky, like write themselves a detailed note, the Haitian keeps tabs on each via spiritual surveillance, and anyone that breaks the contract would have a lethal poison dart swiftly deposited in their necks.

So far, this has only happened twice. Fortunately, the people that were informed of the mermaid's location didn't believe it. Still, it remains a risk. But for the most part, the clients do not want to blow a good thing, anyway, so maintaining her privacy serves their selfish interests as well. Nobody satisfies their deepest, darkest desires like the mermaid. They all merrily drown in her delectable decadence.

The mermaid and the Haitian are able to maintain this lavish lifestyle due to both the steady income from her prostitution but also the treasure she brought up from Atlantis, a trove of diamonds and pearls that the Haitian routinely sells for cash. This was how they purchased this luxurious penthouse.

Decades ago, the mermaid met the Haitian on the beach of his native land. They immediately fell in love. She proposed her plan to live in human society as a professional love-maker, and he helped her by discreetly buying the property, posing as the representative of a wealthy investor. Since the Haitian was paying cash anyway, no further questions were asked.

The penthouse and pool were customized to suit her tastes, and after the Haitian put the word on the street that the fuck of a lifetime could be had at a reasonable rate, her client list was soon long and solid.

Then the vampire shows up and ruins everything.

Reel Three

The vampire hails from Transylvania, and travels around the world only at night, incognito. He, too, has a helpful assistant, a horny, deformed dwarf whose only desire is to make love to the women the vampire victimizes, preferably while they are still alive. The victims are so mesmerized following their lovemaking with the vampire that they do not resist, still under the vampire's spell, oblivious to the dwarf's hideous appearance, in fact turned on by it, ready for more freaky love. This compensates for a life of loneliness on the dwarf's part. The vampire is sympathetic to his plight, and this is his way of providing relief.

When news of Manhattan models being brutally attacked and drained of blood begins making the news, the Haitian becomes alarmed, because he knows the vampire by reputation. Besides being immortal and impervious to conventional methods of death, as the mermaid and the Haitian are, the vampire can also read minds. It would not be long before the vampire becomes aware of the mermaid, and since she indeed offers the epitome of sensual passion, it is inevitable the vampire and his dwarf will want to pay her a call.

The vampire is also extremely handsome and seductive, and furthermore possesses the power to hypnotize anyone who opposes his will. The Haitian fears not even his voodoo magic could stop this undead fiend.

Indeed, even as they discuss this threat, the vampire is stalking the streets of Manhattan, sipping Manhattans in various bars in between drinking blood, resulting in many trips to the bathroom. He scans the minds in every room and eventually, he is able to penetrate the mental fog of a drunken man in a fez, seeing what secrets lie buried deep beneath the fez, discovering to his delight the enticing images of erotic splendor with this most sensuous woman in the world, even if the man in the fez himself is unable to access his own subconscious memories of these tantalizing trysts.

Reel Four

The vampire can never enter any dwelling without an invitation, which is why he hypnotizes the beatnik doorman, telling him to open up and let him in. The dwarf is at his side, rubbing his grubby hands together with lustful anticipation.

The Haitian sees them first and immediately runs up to defend the mermaid, who is resting on the lounge, sipping her Mai Tai. A battle ensues as the mermaid screams, with the Haitian first impaling the vampire with a wooden spear, but in the struggle he misses the heart, and the vampire simply pulls out the weapon from his bloody chest and breaks it in two. Meantime, the dwarf is fondling the mermaid, drooling with desire, while she does her best to fight him off. Finally, the vampire waves his perfectly manicured hand, and with this gesture he instantly robs the Haitian of his voodoo vitality, reducing him to a rotting corpse, since he is in fact a living zombie. The Haitian's features age rapidly, his face becoming ghastly, the pupils of his eyes turning white as he quickly morphs into a lumbering monstrosity. Worse, he is now under the control of the vampire.

The zombie stands pat, arms folded, as the vampire carefully removes his cape and tuxedo, handing them to the zombie, who gingerly drapes them across a chair. Contrary to media reports, the vampire never takes his victims by force. He doesn't use hypnotism, either. The fact is, he is so supernaturally charismatic that no woman, or man, can resist his charms. Due to his aristocratic breeding, he is simply too much of a gentleman to insinuate himself on the unwilling. Of course, this is easy, since they are *all* willing. The mermaid is smitten despite her reservations, especially considering the current state of her Haitian lover, so she spreads out her tail fins and opens her arms anyway. The vampire climbs on top of her, fucking her first gently then furiously as he sinks his fangs into her throat. After he is finished, the dwarf takes his turn, but this time, there is a twist: the vampire has already fallen in love with the mermaid, for the first time in ages, in fact since that werewolf in Transylvania during the previous century, who fell victim to a silver bullet fired by the werewolf's jealous boyfriend. So for this rare occasion, the vampire has purposely transformed the mermaid into one of his own, creating a unique inter-species hybrid. After the drooling dwarf climaxes inside of her, slobbering and weeping with ecstasy, the vampire mermaid viciously tears out his throat, and gore splatters all over her milky, shapely torso.

Confused and crying out in agony, the dwarf rolls around on the hardwood floor, bleeding out and dying, demanding to know why the vampire had allowed this to happen, claiming prejudice against little people. The vampire responds that he did not allow it, he made it happen, because now he has a more powerful assistant in the zombie, so the dwarf's services are no longer required. It has nothing to do with height, the vampire insists, though the charge has shaken his sense of fairness and integrity. Perhaps he was too impulsive. Too late now. The dwarf was a degenerate, anyway, the vampire thinks with uneasy dismissiveness.

The vampire mermaid is gently lifted up by the zombie—who is now also in love with the vampire, and hoping for a threesome at some point—and carried out of the penthouse and down to the vampire's waiting limousine below. The zombie has become his new chauffeur, also an upgrade since the poor dead dwarf had trouble reaching the pedals. All passersby are hypnotized by the vampire, so they do not witness this alarming spectacle of monsters roaming Manhattan.

The vampire takes his mermaid bride to his lair on the outskirts of the city, a dark old mansion, which also has an indoor pool, though it is filled with blood, not saltwater. Though his services as a bodyguard and driver are still required, the zombie is treated as an equal in this household, with the same privileges, especially when its comes to Love. The vampire promises them both he will procure lovers for them from now on, and they'll never have to worry about any of their secrets being revealed, since their lovers will also be their food...*and they all lived happily ever after*!

Reel Five

An Asian woman who resembles the mermaid wakes up in a cot, inside a tiny tenement on the Lower East Side. The camera pans the stark, barren walls of the unkept room, the kitchen sink filled with dirty dishes, clothes strewn across the floor, dead flowers in a vase.

There is a knock on the door. A man who looks like Haitian walks in and strikes her. He is her pimp, and she is his prostitute.

The prostitute pleads with her pimp to stop beating her, but to no avail. He is crying as he hits her, because secretly, he is in love with her. He hates that she has sex with so many strangers for money. He blames himself for her plight, but she is both willing and able, for whatever reason, which only makes him resent her more. When he beats her, it is an act of misdirected self-loathing. But he never wants to be poor again, having endured an impoverished childhood in Harlem. After taking all her cash from a cookie jar, he leaves, swearing profusely and profanely, wiping the tears from his cheeks.

The Asian beauty goes to a cabinet and pulls out a gun. Then she follows her pimp down the hallway, calling out his name. He turned slowly, with resignation, because he knows this moment has finally come, and he is ready. He does not move or resist. Shaken with sobs, she shoots him square in the forehead, blowing out the back of his skull. She falls to her knees, weeping, because in a way, she had loved him too. He was the only lover who could bring her to climax, and make her feel loved, at least briefly.

Sirens wail in the background, but not the kind of sirens from her imaginary home beneath the sea. Still weeping, the sad Asian beauty runs down the stairs and out into the busy city street, pursued by police and an angry mob.

A man resembling the vampire in her fantasy suddenly grabs her and pulls her into an alley. He is the long-lost love of her life, a sailor who had inadvertently broken her heart after the war ended, disappearing without a trace or note, setting her on this miserable path to ruin and shame.

He kisses her and begs her forgiveness, claiming he was afraid of how society would judge their mixed marriage. She embraces him and accepts his apology, as well as his proposal for marriage.

But just then an overly eager, trigger-happy and frankly bigoted rookie police officer shows up and shoots her in the back without warning, consumed by the bitterness he has felt since he was a little boy discovering his father had perished in the Japanese sneak attack on Pearl Harbor. The bullet passes through her and her long-lost love as well. They die together in each other's arms, both victims of a war that never really ended.

Final shot: a closeup of the woman's smile, even as blood trickles from her dead lips. Her real dream had finally come true, if only for a moment.

The End

BIG BUST AT THE CHA CHA LOUNGE

I feel like I'm retired from a career I never had. My name isn't important. Only famous people have names that matter. Everybody else, including me, is a nobody. See, when famous people die, everyone hears about it, and collectively grieve, or celebrate, depending on the person's contributions to the culture. When the rest of us die, hardly anybody notices or cares.

I hate being a nobody, even if most people are, too. There's no comfort in that kind of company. Commiserating is for suckers.

Once, long ago, I was a private eye spying on forbidden liaisons, masturbating with voyeuristic license to the illicit sights and immoral sounds and later, the photographic evidence. Then I walked dogs, still picking up shit for a living. I still miss all those dogs, wherever they are.

I have this vision I'm in Windermere Park in Seattle on an overcast morning, just after dawn, the fog and clouds reflecting softly off the sparkling, silvery waters of Lake Washington, and all the dogs I've ever walked, and all the cats I've ever owned, come running to greet me as celestial synthesizer music swells. It makes me cry, but whether they're tears of joy or grief, I cannot discern. It doesn't matter, because it's cathartic. The music sounds like "3.9_3-wo-ai-ni.0cc," from Volume 6 of the soundtrack to *Mr. Robot*, by Mac Quayle. I down-loaded it to my brain once, and apparently it seeped into my soul.

I often think of the people who have hired me to

walk their dogs. The woman who suddenly left her job at a strip club, for instance. I think of her often.

Right now I'm watching this guy sitting across from my booth, all alone, like me. He keeps scrolling through the camera roll on his phone, from what I can tell, as if searching for evidence of existence. Any existence, outside of this one. I wish I could tell him, but it's against the rules. Plus he wouldn't believe me, anyway.

Once I was down in Gig Harbor, sitting in a dockside cafe, and this older but attractive woman was also sitting there, looking forlorn. My curiosity and other senses somewhat aroused, I went up to her and asked her what was wrong. "Time," she said. "It's too fast for me. I can't catch up. I've been left behind." I understood, and walked away, leaving her alone, since solitude is preferable over random company. The inner void only aches that much more when one's private pain is infringed upon by well-meaning but bothersome strangers.

That's why I don't approach the beautiful young women in this bar. They can't even see me, anyway. I'm invisible to them. As for me, I can look, but I can't touch, even though I am always touched by their presence, dear. God, I loved Blondie. Still do. The band, not the comic strip, though that was okay, too. I miss everything, basically.

Speaking of sassy blonde chanteuses, Peggy Lee is now singing "Fever" as Bettie Page and Tempest Storm and Lili St. Cyr dance along, seemingly, their voluptuous visages immortalized in lurid color on the pulldown screen covering the back wall of the room. As usual it's the burlesque film *Teaserama* (1954), which this bar always plays in a silent loop for background ambience. It went well with the all the vintage *lucha libra* iconography, images of El Santo, Blue Demon and Mil Mascaras, and even the black velvet painting of Laura Palmer from *Twin Peaks*. It was the world inside my head, made manifest, and anyone could visit it. Even me.

This is when Bettie walks off the screen and sits next to me.

"Hello," she says. "I remember you. You're here often."

"I'm everywhere sometimes, but most of the time I'm nowhere."

"What's your name again?"

"I don't remember. Does it matter?"

"I guess not. You know mine, right?"

"Everyone does."

"Not everyone. Hardly anyone anymore, in fact."

"Don't say that. You're a legend. Immortal."

"No, I had my time. But it's over. Now I'm just a ghost on the wall."

"We all are, eventually. At least you had a name once."

"I suppose. It didn't do much for me while I had it. More now that I don't need it anymore."

"Posterity is a myth, an illusion created for those who think they can immortalize their brief existence here in the minds of those that follow."

"Wow. That's pretty good. Who said that?"

"I did. Just now."

I look up at Tempest on the screen, and she winks back at me. She has my number, all right.

"Man, that Tempest has some big boobs," I say.

Bettie looks down at her own chest, and says, "Sorry I don't."

"It's just flesh. It all rots. You know that."

Her eyes moisten, and I feel bad.

"Oh, c'mon. You know you were always my favorite. The most beautiful woman in the world to me, next to my wife. Can't beat those pretty feet, either. *Both* of you. You know I'm a foot man from way back."

"But we never even met. Till now, that is."

"Certainly feels like we have, many times."

"Because you conjured me in your imagination."

"True. But you're just like I imagined you."

"Because you're still imagining me."

Then she's gone. Tempest is no longer winking back at me. I am invisible again.

Sadly, I look around at the young hipsters suddenly flooding the bar, and feel ancient and irrelevant. But then I always have, even when I was young and part of the action. I'm a born anachronism.

I was hoping to find something, or someone, here. I can't recall who. It's like I'm on a case again, back in the old days. Not necessarily the good old days. Okay, some were good. Most, in fact. Now they're all just old.

As usual, I don't know what I am doing here, or anywhere. I have no sense of purpose, no reason for being. I am just drifting from one place to the next, driven by the breeze of whimsy. Whose whimsy, I can't tell you. Maybe just mine. But there is no plan, no pattern, no pain. I am just waiting for the lights to go out. But they never do.

This is so not what I expected.

When I was a private eye—I mean with a license, on active duty—I was always trying to solve mysteries, but they were all finite distractions from long-term existential issues, with no lingering consequences, beyond this transitory realm, anyway. I got old trying to figure out what to do with my youth. Once I realized I wasn't going to be here forever, it felt like it was almost over, and I'd run out the clock trying to figure out a way to beat it.

So now I just float around, encountering others both like me and nothing like me, and some in between. They all exist in a sort of twilight, stuck between two worlds, different eras, not really fitting into any specific time or place, eternally on the outside looking in at those that are either frantically trying to stay in, or desperately trying to get out.

Nothing worked out like I thought it would. I wonder if anything works out for anyone the way they planned. It seems like nothing turns out as good or bad as you hoped or feared. All my dreams went up in smoke, and my pilot light lost its flame, then I burnt out. But maybe that's why dreams are called dreams. They aren't meant to be real.

At least I finally got to meet Elvis. Sinatra, too. Even Marilyn Monroe. She's not so sad anymore.

Sorry I'm talking so much. I have no one else to talk to anymore. Nobody that listens, anyway. I don't even think they can hear me anymore. But that's okay. It makes me feel like I can infiltrate any crowd, anywhere, and not be noticed, or bothered. I'm a spy in the field, with no higher authority to report or answer to. Besides you, that is. But that's my own choice. I'm a truly secret agent, operating autonomously, still trying to uncover the ultimate truth, even if it's right in my face.

Wait, where was I? Oh, yeah. *Here*. For now, anyway. I've lost all sense of time, and Time lost track of me long ago. We don't miss each other.

Man, I love bars, even if I can't drink like I once did. I just dig the ambience of certain joints. I still hang out at "Space Bar," as I call it, the back part of Bar House in the Fremont district of Seattle, the last place I lived. The retro-galaxy wall paintings bathed in black light have particular resonance with me now. It's like the *noir* version of *Forbidden Planet* (1956). I also frequent the Ballard Smoke Shop, where my wife and I often went for french fries and Martinis, followed by Mai Tais at Betty's Room in the Sunset Tavern next door. If I'm not in Ballard, you could look for me (but not actually find me) at the Unicorn across the street from where I am now, or the Lost Lake Lounge just up the street. (I used to frequent the Wedgwood Broiler, but I had a fling with a waitress there that went sour after she was repelled by my foot fetish, so I avoid it now). They're all so cozy and timeless. Though it's all timeless to me from this dreamy, detached vantage point. The entire Universe is just an intra-dimensional Salvador Dali painting to me now. I jump into black holes (actually time portals) dotting the vast, barren, surrealistic space-scape to visit memories and places of my distant past, inhabiting them for a short time, always making new observations and taking notes like I did when on the trail of a mark back in my P.I. days, before being pulled back into the vortex of eternity, caught in a continual loop of floating stasis and perpetual nostalgia and virtual voyeurism. I can see everything everyone is doing, but from a healthy distance, so I can make objective commentary to share with you. I can't interpret the information I gather in the field, though. That's all up to you. I've earned my own eternity-weary wisdom and omnipotent perspective the hard way. Wait for your turn.

But I must admit one thing: now that I have all the answers, I wish I had more questions. Not that anyone asked me, but the only advice I have to offer is this: sometime, when you're in a bad mood and hating your life, pause and imagine that this moment actually happened long, long ago, and you've been given permission to randomly revisit it from some dark, distant future, when you're old or sick or dead. Trust me, it will help you appreciate maybe not that particular moment, but all the moments surrounding it, the stuff you took for granted, the proverbial little things, whether it's someone's face or the music on the radio or the taste of a favorite snack or the color of the sky or the loved one waiting for you at home, even if it's just a pet. Suddenly what seemed like the worst day of your life might instead be appreciated as just another one of those good old days, with just a few bad moments mixed because that's the way of the world. Whatever it is, good or bad, it won't last anyway, except as a memory. Just try it. Trust me.

Now Esquivel is playing. I've always loved Esquivel. Great music never dies. Only those that make it.

You see, whoever you are, this is what it is: the Cha Cha Lounge was one of my favorite haunts when I was still alive, meaning inside a physical form. And all these many, many years or eons or whatever later, it remains one of my favorite haunts. It's exactly like I remember it, too. Because it's no longer actually there, either. Long gone, just like me. An intangible memory trapped in ethereal amber. Like you, someday. If you see me, please don't bug me. I prefer being alone until I can find my wife, and all those missing dogs and cats. I know they're out there, somewhere, waiting for me. I can feel them.

Despite finally unraveling the mysteries of the Universe, I'm the one who's still lost.

HUNT, KILL, FEED, FUCK. REPEAT.

The creatures followed only their primal instincts in pursuit of their own short-term survival, fornicating without propagation, existing without living, oblivious to the raging nightmares inevitably replacing their complacent little dreams.

The human race would once do things like gloat with ethical pride while reading the news about the government outlawing "animal cruelty" over a steak dinner or bacon breakfast or hamburger lunch, an official act of pseudo-benevolence contrived mainly to absolve our society of guilt. Or at least the feeling of guilt. Among most of humanity, empathy for fellow sentient beings that did not share their physical or mental characteristics was not deemed necessary for moral self-aggrandizement.

Then it all changed, suddenly, relentlessly, and irrevocably. First the outbreaks started in remote communities, then spread to larger urban centers, simultaneously around the globe, which was already threatened with final destruction due to manmade catastrophes, big and small. Society was eating itself alive. Literally.

After the fires and floods and droughts induced by climate change inexplicably instigated the once-mythical zombie apocalypse, the animal kingdom rose up in uniform resurrection, since they now outnumbered their human oppressors, and realized collectively they no longer had to take this shit anymore, being hunted and bred and slaughtered by the billions for centuries, recycled as food and clothes and other disposable goods. Now when the remainder of humanity ventured out into the ravaged wilderness to seek sustenance and shelter, the beasts stalked and devoured them, at least the ones that somehow managed to escape the ravenous hordes of their undead counterparts.

The lingering human survivors no longer marked time. Acknowledging the passing of a day or month or year or decade only illuminated the inevitable fact that by the end of that day or month or year or decade, they'd all likely be dead. Of course, the elders among them had stopped noticing the calendar long before all this happened. The assaultive series of natural and unnatural and supernatural catastrophes, which all seemed like the inevitable results of self-inflicted fatal wounds in a mass suicide, evened the stakes and flattened the field for everyone, regardless of age, fitness, heritage, faith or economic status. The blackness that beckoned to them from beyond this waking nightmare was too terrifying to contemplate, and that unifying, uniform fear of being alone and unconscious forever undermined their instincts for basic survival. Thus they were collectively reduced to existing for its own sake amid all this unrelenting horror and unmitigated misery. The malaise that engulfed and consumed and permeated their consciousness had become the normal state of being, and they clung to it desperately, since it beat the single alternative. Their only relative relief was in gratuitous sensual indulgence.

Scarce remnants of so-called civilization were holed up at the charmingly rustic and woodsy Kalaloch

Lodge on the edge of the majestic rainforests in Olympic National Park, Washington, located against the scenic, rocky, driftwood-littered shore of the Pacific Coast. Bored and depressed, but somehow still hungry and horny, they were simply drinking and fornicating the rest of their dwindling lives away.

The group occupying the Kalaloch Lodge had no way of knowing if anyone else of their kind existed. There was no Internet, no cell phone coverage, no television or radio signals. They did have electricity, so for diversion they were forced to watch the stack of DVDs recovered from an abandoned library in Port Angeles over and over. Ironically, the titles included *Day the World Ended* (1955), *Day of the Animals* (1977), and *Day of the Dead* (1985). In the attic of a deserted mid-century home that had briefly served as their sanctuary they also discovered copies of *Playboy Magazine* from the 1960s, and issues of black-and-white monster comics from the 1970s like *Tales of the Zombie, Eerie, Creepy*, and *Vampirella,* all of which fueled their fevered fantasies, while eerily reflecting the world around them.

There were just five still left alive here: three women and two men. The two men were a hunky firefighter and an escaped convict who was ugly but virile. The three women were a nurse who luckily happened to be a nymphomaniac, a sexy hippie social worker who liked hiking which was how she got stuck here, and a buxom, matronly politician that had been on a solitary vacation, to just get away from it all, till it all followed her. They could be considered representatives of an eclectic society that no longer existed, but that would be too obvious. And they weren't nearly diverse enough.

Since they were outnumbered, the men were often outvoted when it came to matters of entertainment agenda, food distribution, and other minor, now meaningless details of this make- believe microcosm of a polite, organized social structure. The men didn't care who called the shots as long as they got regular sex. The social worker was bi-sexual, so she often only had sex with the other women. The two men had sex with the nurse and the politician and occasionally the social worker when she was tired of pussy. The nympho nurse was the most conventionally attractive, the hippie social worker the most open-minded, and the politician the most experienced. The men were merely functional pieces of meat. It worked in the end. And this was The End, so no reason to haggle.

Even though the lodge's booze supply was running low, and the nearest hint of civilization was miles and miles away, through the dangerous forest, they decided to have a 1950s themed cocktail party, playing old LPs (also found in that mid-century house) by Esquivel, Les Baxter, Henry Mancini, Frank Sinatra, Dean Martin, Julie London, Sarah Vaughan, June Christy, Ella Fitzgerald, and other lounge and jazz artists. In the closets of the cabins and rooms they had dis-covered some suitable wardrobe that, while not period specific, suited the makeshift classy occasion. It was all an illusion anyway. Might as well make it stylish and comfortable, they figured.

The main lodge was where they congregated, but each occupied their own private seaside cabin. Whenever they decided to retire to their personal retreats, they had to make a run for it, and sometimes they were pursued by zombies or animals still trying to take them down. Fortunately they were well armed, having stocked multiple weapons from various abandoned military sites and police stations, and were able to fend off any stray attackers. It was worth the extra effort, because being cooped up together eventually made them hate each other. They all needed a break sometimes. The cabins were the obvious solution. This is where they ether individually or occasionally paired off and spent time reflecting and remembering, mourning their previous routines, even the arduous aspects of it, since at least it sustained a trance that allowed them to ignore their own mortality. Now that distraction had been removed from the equation of consciousness, terminally distant from a world preoccupied with power and money and petty social media disputes and sports and movies. Now all that remained was that most ancient of anxiety cures, sex. While poking and probing and penetrating each other's bodies, they were able to mentally block out the fact that these vessels were like machines about to be tossed on the junk pile. They were never built to last, anyway. And when they broke down, whatever these things called "personality" and "identity" were would probably go with them. These bodies were their only connections to consciousness, so they clung to these doomed disguises as if they was their only hope for immortality, at least the illusion of it.

Now with death stalking them literally night and day, and having been driven to the edge of the land itself, with no place else to run or hide, trapped forever or at least until their bodies shut down within the luxurious confines of a cozy resort that felt more like a prison, they were constantly confronted with the harsh, violent reality undermining their sense of a safe sanctuary. It was all going to end, probably suddenly and painfully, and there was no way to avoid it, except with momentary self-delusion.

Peggy Lee was singing "Is That All There Is?" as the final five tried to make the best of their dire situation, even as the wailing and moans of the encroaching undead and the savage beasts echoed throughout the wilderness around them. The Pacific Ocean was their only escape route, but they had no marine transportation. So this was it.

Now Dave Brubeck was playing "Take Five." Other than random small talk and reminiscing about the good old days which were any old days from this perspective, the group still tried to figure out the cause of their sad and strange circumstances.

It doesn't matter who's saying what, because they're all saying the same things:

"I wonder why the zombies don't eat the animals. Only us."

"Because they're cannibals."

"Ironic. We ate animals when we were alive, but when we're dead, we only eat our own."

"I guess maybe we should've done that before it was too late. Harvesting all those farm animals for food was bad for the environment, and the world was overpopulated. Cannibalism might've saved our species."

"Was it even worth saving?"

"Apparently not. The animals are doing much better without us. The zombies have mostly starved to death. Soon we'll join them, and then we'll starve to death, too."

"So we'll die twice. Also ironic."

"How so."

"Since we only live once."

"Or twice, if you're James Bond."

"You're not."

"It's a good thing we had zombie movies. Otherwise we wouldn't have known what those things were."

"And we have electricity. In all the zombie movies, people still had working electricity. Amazing."

"And no bills to pay."

"That's the beauty of it."

"Life imitating art. Well, if you can call it art."

"Depends on the director."

"All of Romero's rules came true."

"Shots to the head worked, anyway. There were just too damn many of them, all at once. And then the animals turned on us. We ran out of ammo, surrounded and outnumbered. We never stood a chance. I don't know why we don't just blow our brains out. Kill two birds with one stone, since we won't come back that way with a head wound."

"I used to love the sounds of birds. Now they terrify me."

"Hitchcock tried to warn us."

"I still love animals, even if they hate us. I was fucking vegan. I don't deserve their animosity."

"Well, you're still here, so maybe they sensed that."

"Then why are you still here?"

"Good point, but then you're no longer vegan, either."

"True. But I try."

"Too late. We all gotta go. It's like a, whaddyacallit in law…"

"Rico case."

"Right. Rico case. We're all guilty of mass murder."

"We were all born innocent."

"Nobody dies innocent, though."

"Such a shame so many animals died in the fires and floods and droughts before the zombies took over the planet and set things right for them."

"Yeah. Hard for me to feel pity now, though. I wish they'd all been burned, even if it destroyed Earth's entire ecosystem. Pretty soon they'll be the only ones who will benefit from it, anyway."

"Maybe that's how it was meant to be. Mankind was an extraneous overreach of evolution, a fatal virus, and Nature finally purged us from her planet."

"What about our contributions to culture at least? Music, cinema, literature, the arts?"

"I dig jazz, so I'll give you that much."

"Science, technology?"

"Meh. Fat lotta good that did us in the end."

"Politics, religion."

"You're losing me."

"Ultimately all of these ingenious inventions proved to be mere distractions from the inevitable, meaning both our individual and collective demise, so they were simply self-serving."

"Fuck you, hippie."

"Maybe later. I only eat live sausage."

"Face it. We deserve this."

"Still sucks."

"It sucks most species were wiped off the face of

the planet."

"Including ours."

"But we were the custodians. It was our responsibility to protect the others."

"Other what?"

"Living things."

"Oh, fuck that hippie shit. You think earthquakes and hurricanes and plagues and cancer discriminate with any sense of justice? It was all fucked from the beginning. We've just been reduced to what we were before we were able to build these towns and cities and arenas and theaters and restaurants and all the other things that made us believe we'd live forever, as if this was all there was. Now we know *this* is all there really is, stripped of civilization. And it won't even be here that long, not in the scheme of things."

"Except we turned out to be the worst plague."

"You just hate people."

"I do."

"I'm so glad I never had the need to breed."

"I miss my kids, my family."

"So do I."

"I'm glad I don't have one to miss."

"We're your family now."

"I know. How sad."

"It's really all over, isn't it? I just can't accept that, even though it's unavoidable."

"It all ends for each of us eventually. Might as well just get the inevitable over with."

"I'd rather die peacefully in my sleep."

"We're all asleep. It's just a dream."

"Nightmare. Endless nightmare."

"There's nothing left for us out there. No hopes, no

aspirations. No dreams. We're dead inside already, just waiting for the outside to catch up."

"Maybe it's for the best. It's the mystery that makes life interesting, anyway."

"No mysteries left. It's all been reduced to its basic core elements."

"Sex and death."

"Exactly. The beginning and end of all flesh."

"Even the animals are out there, fighting and feeding and fucking."

"That's because they only run on instinct. They're not capable of making conscientious choices."

"Except to suddenly decide *en masse* to attack humans."

"That's been a long time coming. Basic survivalism."

"I wonder if they can't see the distinction between zombies and humans, and so they felt this was the thing to do."

"Frankly, I don't see the distinction either, so I can't blame them."

"At least the climate seems rebalanced, without all our toxins poisoning the environment."

"Fuck that hippie shit. Who cares about natural beauty if no one is here to enjoy it?"

"The animals."

"Ah, they don't care. You really think they give a shit about hippie eye candy?"

"Plus they're part of the natural beauty."

"So is my body, baby."

"I dig."

"Maybe some art, true *art,* doesn't need appreciation from outsiders. It exists for its own sake."

"Like we do."

"Did."

"I appreciate your body. Every night."

"Thanks, I appreciate your appreciation. Get it while it lasts."

"Maybe there are others out there, like us. We can't lose hope."

"Hope for what? Even if was all a dream, we're just gonna wake up and die anyway."

"This is the mystery I was talking about."

"Only one way to really solve it. You ready?"

"No. There are other mysteries I'd rather investigate first, that at least have short term solutions not requiring my immediate sacrifice."

"I heard there was a race of people living in those forests who averaged only twelve inches."

"*Ooo!*"

"In *height*."

"Oh."

"I wish one of us was a scientist. Or at least religious. Instead we're just a bunch of unemployed hedonists doomed to sudden death any minute."

"As Nature originally intended before we made it complicated."

"I'm so drunk. Wanna fuck again while I'm still awake?"

"Sure."

Their collective existential malaise was returning, despite the forced revelry, spoiling the mood and ruining the party.

Eventually, as the night wore on and a storm brewed, they all wound up in a single beach cabin after outrunning a sudden wave of vicious monsters. The zombies and animals and stormy weather beat up against the wooden walls and windowpanes, but the structure remained stead-fast.

Convinced this was their last stand, they all began to fuck each other, even man on man, since the carnal pleasures of this realm would soon be denied them forever, so it was all precious. Their naked skin was soaked with semen, vaginal juices, saliva, and even blood as the primal ferocity of their passions in the face of impending oblivion dominated their senses. Their deep disdain for one another also contributed to the sheer intensity of the mutual carnage.

That's when they began to eat each other, resorting to the cannibalism that might've once saved their species from extinction. Their gnawing hunger after rationing what little food remained overwhelmed them, and their time was finally running out, so they feasted on raw human flesh, like all those stories of plane crash survivors turning on each other in remote, snowbound mountains. It had been done before, so precedent justified their behavior, at least to them. Except they ate each other alive. Their screams drowned out the sounds from the things still engulfing the isolated cabin here on the brink of mankind's extinction.

They woke up together in a single bed, naked and covered in bodily fluids, most not their own. The evidence of the debauchery was strewn across the cabin: empty booze bottles, broken cocktail glasses, half-eaten food, discarded clothing.

Outside it was quiet. But the silence was serene and soothing, not eerie and foreboding.

Bloodshot eyes squinting in the pale sunlight

beaming through the drapes of the beachside cabin, they all peeked outside to tentatively observe the current state of their situation.

A deer and a bear were grazing the brilliantly green grass peacefully, side by side. Rabbits hopped about happily. There was no sign of aggression, even between the beasts.

1950s/'60s-era cars were parked alongside the main lodge. It was all a display for a vintage seaside show, apparently. Elvis Presley sang "Follow That Dream" over the booming sound system. Bright, happy, well-dressed people of all colors and ages were gathering about, frolicking in the sunshine, laughing and eating and drinking and enjoying the dawn of a new day in their fabricated paradise.

Finally, seemingly overnight, humanity, or what remained of it, had learned to peacefully coexist.

No zombies were in sight. At least not now. Not yet. The sky was painted a deep blue, augmented by fluffy cumulous clouds. A soft breeze wafted in off the ocean. Seagulls flew about, ignoring the fish just below the pristine surface. There was even a fucking rainbow.

The five felt consumed with shame, at least at first. But then they were emboldened by other emotions, protective of what they'd claimed as their own. They wondered who all these intrusive assholes were, and if they had polished off their stash of booze and food. Something might have to be done. Meantime, they could shoot and eat the rabbits. And if these strangers gave them any resistance, they'd be shot, too. In the head. Just in case.

Guns in hand, cocked and loaded, they left the cabin and rejoined civilization. For whatever reason, they'd been given a second chance. This time they'd make sure to strike first. Others would join their cause, for they'd seen the future, and would share the opportunity to change mankind's fate. Even if everyone was eventually going to die of something, anyway. Meantime, it was one big party. Invitation only. Interlopers not welcome on their turf, which they would defend against all threats from now on.

Had it all been a fever dream? That was the only answer. But the question remained: *what caused the fever?*

You got me, Peggy Lee.